POLLY's
HOMECOMING

(A Sequel to Polly's Small Town War)

by

J.E. Christer

For My Grandchildren

With Love

ONE

November 1946

Polly and Christopher Beauchamp alighted from the train in Barton upon Humber on a foggy, damp day. The heady mixture of steam and soot failed to move far, held captive by the fog. It engulfed them both, causing Polly to cough a little. She smiled at her husband as they waited for their bags. She was home at last. She hugged herself, eyes shining with excitement, as she looked around. She'd try and remember this moment forever – her homecoming. After spending almost six years in Canada where Chris had been seconded during the war to train pilots, Polly was glad to be home and excited about seeing family. She would soon see her sister, Laura, her husband, George, and of course little Emma, their child.

Chris smiled at her obvious joy, "Come on, dreamy head. Let's see Mr Osgood about getting these bags taken to the Elms. I'll tell him to bring them round in a couple of hours, after we've been to see Laura and George."

Polly twirled around in a circle, causing her shiny, dark hair to fly out behind her. She grinned widely, arms outspread, "I'm so happy to be back, Chris. The old place doesn't look any different, does it?"

Chris looked around and agreed that as far as he could see, fog permitting, it looked the same as always. After giving instructions to Mr Osgood about delivery of their bags, they set off towards Humber Terrace, where Laura and George had been forced to move since the owners of their old place had given them notice. The bomb damage in Hull was extensive and their landlords had needed the accommodation for themselves. Polly and Laura had exchanged letters as frequently as possible, but the war years had been long, and post was often lost in transit for one reason or another, but at least they had the new address.

As they passed the Ropery on their right, they could hear muted shouts of the men unloading sisal from the boats on the River Haven. St. Chad's church looked lonely and forlorn on its plot opposite as it watched from sightless windows the comings and goings of human endeavours. The landscape was flat and, lost in the mist, whilst the Humber estuary flowed silently, its grey waters reflecting the fog-bound sky.

***

Laura Taylor opened the back door of her end-terraced house. She was half expecting it to be one of George's sisters coming to see how he was after his latest bout of illness. Instead, she had the surprise of her life when she looked up to see Polly and Chris, standing there grinning from ear to ear.

"Surprise!" they shouted together and Polly held her arms out to her sister who immediately walked into them in a daze of pleasure.

"Come in, come in," she ushered them both into the kitchen and closed the door. In the left corner of the room the fireplace was smoking badly with sub-standard coal but now and again, a glimmer of flame flickered through. Occasionally, the fire spat out sparks as if it had indigestion, and the pock-marked lino bore witness to this with small burnt holes within spitting distance of the grate.

"I can't believe it's really you, Polly, and you, Chris." Her eyes swept over them as she tried to take in every detail.

"Well, it is us, our Laura. Is the kettle on? We could murder a decent cuppa."

Laura tried to take their coats, hug them again, and put the kettle on all at once. Polly laughed at her sister who was usually so calm and collected. She held her still saying, "You put the kettle on and we'll take care of the coats."

Laura smiled and took a deep breath, "You've completely taken the wind out of my sails. I'd no idea you were coming home."

"We didn't want to spoil the surprise," Chris said. Their conversation was halted momentarily when they heard a thud from upstairs.

"That's George. He's been a bit poorly," Laura explained in hushed tones. "I'll just go and see if he's able to come down and see you." She paused and looked back into the room, "You'll find he's changed a lot since you last saw him."

Polly's face fell, "Oh, I'm sorry, Laura. Tell you what, I'll make the tea. You go and see to George."

As Laura disappeared upstairs, Polly filled the kettle and placed it on the stove. She was thrilled to see Laura, but saw a change in her since they had left in 1941. She looked care-worn and tired behind her happy facade. Her hair no longer shone and it was cut in a severe style, making her face thinner and her features sharper.

She could hear mumbled voices and a creaking of bed springs, followed by slow footfalls on the stairs. Then Laura, helping George, who was wearing his old brown and grey plaid dressing gown, appeared in the kitchen.

A few minutes later they were sat around the fire in the living room, which was burning brighter than the one in the kitchen, and Polly was shocked to see how ill George had become. "What does the doctor say about your illness? Are you going to get better soon?"

"Doctors, what do they know?" George looked into the fire with derision. "He says I picked up malaria and dysentery in Burma, as if I didn't already know."

"But you *will* get better, won't you?" Polly looked from Laura to George and back again for confirmation.

"He's already getting better," Laura replied. She looked at George, "Aren't you, love?"

"So he says, but he's not laid in bed like an invalid for weeks on end, is he?"

"I'm sure you'll soon be on the mend, George," Polly smiled, trying to inject some hope into the situation. "And if we can do anything....."

"We don't need anybody's charity, thank you very much."

"I didn't mean that." Polly looked anxiously at Chris who shuffled uncomfortably in his seat.

"I think what Polly meant......" Chris began.
George cut him off, "Leave it. I'll be up and about soon and start looking for a job. We can manage."

Polly looked at Laura whose face showed the strain she was under, "Where's Emma?" she asked to ease the tension.

"She's at school now."

"Yes, of course, I'd forgotten how time flies. She must be six years old."

"She goes to the Church school, just like we did."

"I remember the fire in the hearth in the infant's classroom. It was always warm in that room but the rest of the place was freezing in the winter."

"It hasn't changed at all, Polly, except that Miss Hewitt's retired now and a Mr Ross has taken over as headmaster. He seems alright and I think he's able to control the boys better than Miss Hewitt did."

"I can't wait to see Emma. I bet she won't remember her Aunt Polly, will she?"

"Don't you believe it," Laura replied and rolled her eyes. "She's always asking me to tell her stories of when we were little girls. Now you can tell them to her yourself and give me a rest. Every time a letter came with a Canadian stamp on it I had to read it to her at least ten times."

Polly smiled. She was relieved to hear that Emma knew of her. She had been a toddler when she and Chris had left for Canada. Now five years had passed and they hadn't been blessed with children themselves which cut at her heart every time she thought about it.

Laura jumped up, "Come into the kitchen and we'll make that tea everyone is gasping for. The kettle should be boiling by now. You can tell me about your journey back."

Grateful for the excuse to leave the room for a moment, Polly stood up. Chris reached for her hand and squeezed it.

With the women out of the way in the kitchen, George looked at Chris with as much grace as he could manage, "You're looking well, Chris. Canada must have done you good."

"Yes, I was one of the lucky ones. It must have been hell for you. I'm so sorry, George, I almost feel guilty for not suffering with you."

"Yes, well, I suppose it could have been worse for me too, remember. At least I came home – thousands didn't."

"It's good of you to look at it like that. Many would say that it was my privileged upbringing that got me out at the right time, but believe it or not, it wasn't."

"Just the luck of the draw, Chris – just the luck of the draw. None of us were in control of our lives at the time. We went where we were sent and that's just how it was, so don't go feeling guilty on my account. Anyway, you could have been shot down on any one of your bombing missions so you've had a spell of danger too. Laura's been wonderful and looked after me really well. I'll soon be up and about again."

George reached out to shake Chris's hand in a strong grip. The heat from the living room fire had brought a warm feeling to his cheeks, and he hoped it had got rid of his earlier pallor. They turned their conversation to more mundane matters whilst waiting for the women to bring the tea.

In the kitchen, Laura was entertaining Polly with a description of her neighbours, the Baxters. "I'm telling you, Polly, there are seven families in this terrace and four wash houses so we have allocated days to use the coppers to do the washing, but if Dot Baxter wants to boil her whites then she doesn't care whose day it is, she just goes ahead and uses one. Anyway, tell me about your journey. How long have you been back?"

"We docked at Southampton last night and we've only just got off the train. The luggage was picked up by Betty Osgood's dad at the station and he's taking it to The Elms in an hour or so. We've no idea what the place looks like yet because I just wanted to get to see you again. I've missed you so much, Laura. I found it really hard to settle in Canada. I'm so glad to be home."

This time she could hold the tears back no longer and her face was awash as Laura went to embrace her young sister. "I've missed you too, Polly. That Hitler has a lot to answer for and I hope he's burning in Hell now. I really do."

Polly nodded her agreement and managed a sniff and a small smile. She looked at the clock on the mantelpiece over the fire. It was two o'clock. Laura noticed her glance and added, "We'll just have this cuppa and then you can walk with me to pick Emma up from school if you like."

"I'd love to. We'll walk back to the Elms up Queen Street and see if anything's changed. We'll say 'hello' to Emma and then I'll come back to see you at the weekend to catch up properly. Will that be alright?"

"'Course it will. We can go shopping together like we used to. Nothing's changed though. It's still the same sleepy old Barton that you left five years ago."

When they went back into the sitting room, George and Chris were chatting away happily and Laura noticed how the visit had done her husband good. His eyes were brighter and his face had more colour than she'd seen for weeks. Tea was served with small buns that Laura had baked the day before, and even though it was 1946 and the war had been over for more than a year, some food was still hard to come by and rationing was still in force, but it was getting better week by week.

The next half an hour flew by and Laura stood up to get her coat and boots on to go and fetch Emma from school.

"We'd better be off now, too," Polly said as Chris nodded in agreement.

Chris and Polly took their leave of George, noticing that although he looked better in himself, he was obviously tired by the unexpected conversation. He told Laura he would be waiting up to see Emma and then he would probably go back to bed again.

***

The weather was cold and a bitter north wind had sprung up which was beginning to disperse the fog at least. They walked back down towards the station and then turned left into Butts Lane. "What was the weather like in Canada when you left?" Laura asked.

"The snow was six feet deep in places but you sort of get used to it," Chris replied.

"I don't think I could ever get used to chilblains and frost bite," Laura answered and Polly laughed at the exaggeration.

"It does get very cold there but it seems to be a dry coldness in some ways. Do you think it'll be a hard winter here again?" Polly asked as she drew her scarf around her neck and pushed her arm through Chris's to shield herself from the wind.

"I don't know but I'm going to get Emma some new wellies from Miss Mathers on Saturday. If you don't get them early she'll have sold out."

By this time they had reached the school gates and were stamping their feet to keep out the cold. Emma came running out of the girl's entrance, curly dark hair bouncing as she went. Her curls were inherited from her father, Polly noticed, and a cotton plimsoll bag dangled from one wrist. She stopped abruptly when she saw her mother wasn't alone and Laura laughed at her sudden shyness. She stood with big, brown eyes wide with wonderment as Polly bent down to speak to her.

"Hello, Emma. I'm your Aunt Polly and this is your Uncle Chris. We've come back all the way from Canada to see you and your Mam and Dad."

Emma looked up at Chris and then at her mother, and Laura nodded her confirmation that this was entirely true. She smiled and then put her arms around Polly's neck and gave her a big hug, which almost started Polly crying again. She held onto the child and kissed her little face to cover her emotions. "It's so lovely to see you again, Emma, after all this time. You've really grown into a big girl, haven't you?"

Emma nodded shyly and sought her mother's hand as she pulled away from Polly's embrace. "We're going to be staying here now and we'll be coming to see you again as soon as we're settled in. First though, I want to give you some pennies for some sweets if that's alright with your Mam. Polly looked at Laura who nodded her agreement and Polly put two pennies into the little girl's gloved hand. Emma's eyes widened even more, "Oh, thank you, Aunty Polly. I'll be able to get lots of sweets with this much, won't I, Mam?"

"You'll have to make them last though, Emma," her mother warned.

Chris crouched down to Emma's level and put his hand in his pocket and drew out a silver sixpence and put it inside Emma's glove. "Keep that in your money box and you'll be able to buy some more sweets when your tuppence runs out." Emma moved awkwardly towards Chris, not being used to any other man apart from her dad and gave him a quick hug before returning to her mother.

"Well, we'd better be on our way now. Thanks for the tea, Laura, and we'll see you again soon."

***

Polly linked Chris's arm as they moved away. She was upset at having to say goodbye again, but knew they would have to get back to the Elms to settle in before dark. After goodbye waves they made for the High Street. Laura was right, she thought, the rest of Europe and parts of England may have been laid waste by war, but nothing much had changed in sleepy old Barton.

Polly linked Chris's arm as they moved away. She was upset at having to say goodbye again, but knew they would have to get back to the Elms to settle in before dark. After goodbye waves they made for the High Street. Laura was right, she thought, the rest of Europe and parts of England may have been laid waste by war, but nothing much had changed in sleepy old Barton.

***

Back at the Elms it was a different story. The rooms looked as if bombs had dropped on each one with the remnants of hospital paraphernalia spilling out into corridors and down the stairs. Chris and Polly stood in the hallway and looked around them in horror. It was going to take weeks, if not months, to get the house looking like a home again. Chris opened the door which led down to the kitchen and held Polly's hand as they walked down the short flight of stairs. A scuffling noise and a muttered oath drew their attention to the walk-in pantry at the back of the room. Chris motioned for Polly to stay where she was and he quietly moved in the direction of the noise, only to be brought up short by bumping into Mrs Garside, their family cook before the war. She backed out of the pantry dragging a cardboard box behind her.

"Oh! What the ....?" She turned around quickly and then gave Chris a turn by shouting out loud and flinging her arms around him. "Master Chris, oh, thank goodness it's you. Where did you spring from? Why didn't you let me know you were coming home? Where's Polly?" Her questions were fired like shots from a gun and Polly ran down the rest of the stairs to throw herself into her arms.

"Mrs Garside. It's so wonderful to see you. We thought all the staff had gone when the convalescent home closed." She hugged the older lady until she was begging for mercy but both were tearful at their reunion. Mrs Garside was still a tubby lady despite the deprivations of war and rationing. Her thin, wispy hair frizzed out from beneath a headscarf tied into a turban.

"There's only me left I'm afraid. Mr Harrison retired and moved away to live with his sister in Hornsea, and I've only been coming in occasionally to make sure everything's alright. Ned is too old now to do the garden but Jim might come back if he can."

"We appreciate you coming in once in a while, Mrs Garside. How do you fancy coming back to help us full time?" Chris suggested.

"Just you try stopping me. I might be a bit long in the tooth now, but you can't get rid of me that easy. Say the word and I'll come back tomorrow."

"It'll be like old times, won't it, Mrs Garside?" Polly smiled.

"What were you doing when we came in?" Chris asked.

"I was just trying to tidy up the pantry. I don't think I'll be able to manage everything on my own Master Chris. There's work for an army in the kitchen alone, and then there's the rest of the place." She looked gloomy as she pointed to the range that had once gleamed black and shiny.

"Give me a day or two to catch up with myself, Mrs Garside, and we'll get our Laura to help. We'll soon have it shipshape again."

"I think Laura might have her hands full with George at the moment, Polly," Chris reminded her.

"Oh yes, of course, but she might find an hour or two while he's asleep." Polly felt guilty for forgetting so soon that Laura had her hands full now with her family.

"I think you need some sleep, Polly. We'll tackle the problems one by one and maybe employ some people to help with the clean up. What do you think, Mrs Garside?"

"I know a few women who would jump at the chance of earning a few bob for a week or two. Once it's back to normal it'll be easier to manage and you could employ someone full time then if you wanted to."

"Right, well for now we ought to check out which rooms are habitable upstairs. The private wing should be just as we left it."

Polly felt as if she had been travelling for months instead of days. She was dropping with fatigue as Chris led her through a door marked 'Private' at the top of the stairs. Before turning the house over to the military as a convalescent home, Sir Giles, Chris's father, had insisted that some rooms were kept for family visits. Chris, and his elder brother Martin, had used their old rooms frequently during the earlier part of the war and as he opened his bedroom door he was pleased to see that, although dusty, the room had been left alone.

"I'll need to change the sheets before getting into that bed, Chris. I can't sleep on sheets that haven't been changed for five years. The room needs dusting too," Polly noted as she ran her finger along the top of a tallboy.

"Let's set to it then. There must be some cleaning stuff around here somewhere." He headed out of the door and found a cupboard with clean sheets stacked high on shelves. Underneath the shelves were buckets, dusters and polish so they both tackled the cleaning together and within an hour the room was sparkling again.

"I'm too tired to do the windows tonight. I just want a hot bath and then go to bed".

"I'll check with Mrs Garside that the boiler's been lit. You sit down and I'll be back in a minute."

Chris was doing his best to keep her happy, she knew that, and sat down on the side of the bed. She knew she was being irritable but tried not to take it out on him as he must be tired too, but fatigue overcame her and by the time he came back with clean, fluffy towels and the news that hot water would be available within the hour, Polly was fast asleep on the bed.

TWO

It took a month of hard work from a team of paid and unpaid helpers before The Elms looked anything like its former self. It was almost Christmas before the last of the workers left and Polly could see that although there was still much to be done it was at least clean and habitable once more. Mrs Garside had employed a cleaner to come in once a week to do the heavy work but she insisted that the kitchen remained her own domain. She did relent though when Chris offered to employ a young girl to help out with mundane tasks. After interviewing a few girls, she settled on Joyce Metcalf, who agreed to come in and help on a part-time basis but would remain living at home with her widowed mother.

The weather was cold enough to freeze the water channels leading into the Haven where Laura lived but the boatbuilding continued as it always had. Polly visited her as often as she could and was horrified to hear that the house in Humber Terrace had had to be stoved out before they could live in it because it was alive with fleas. George hadn't earned much money since returning from Burma due to his illnesses, but he hoped to gain employment once he was fit enough. He had been a welder in the shipyards across the water in Hull before the war and hoped to return one day. Laura had managed to get some part-time work at Hoppers making bicycles again and they just about managed to make ends meet.

Their childhood home on Beck Hill had been sold just before the end of the war and the proceeds split between the sisters. Laura was constantly dipping into this reserve to tide them over until George found a decent job and it became a constant source of worry to her. Her once optimistic outlook and demeanour had been replaced by worry lines and despair, which didn't go unnoticed when Polly visited her a week before Christmas. She opened the back door of the house to find Laura on a stool before the small fire in the corner, head bowed and shoulders slumped. She jumped when she heard the door open and quickly wiped her face with her apron, trying to conceal her red eyes while pushing a handkerchief in her pocket as she stood up.

"Oh, Polly, hello love. I wasn't expecting you today. Come in."

"What's wrong, Laura? Is it George? Is Emma alright?"

"Yes, they're fine thanks. Take no notice of me I'm just feeling a bit down in the dumps today."

Polly pulled up another stool and pulled her sister back towards the fire. She reached out to touch Laura's hand and squeezed it gently. "I've just come round to ask if you and George would like to bring Emma to The Elms for Christmas – to stay I mean, not just visit. I thought we could have a real, family Christmas together there and Chris thought we could have a party for New Year. We were planning it last night and thought we might ask all our old friends. You can ask George's family too if you think they'd like it. What do you think, Laura? Will you come?"

"That sounds really lovely, Polly. How long were you thinking we should stay?"

"We thought you might like to come on Christmas Eve and stay until after the party on New Year's Eve. We're planning a lovely New Year's Day dinner. Please say you'll stay, Laura".

"I'll have to ask George of course, but I'm sure Emma would love it."

Polly jumped up laughing and clapping her hands. "Oooh, lovely. I can't wait to tell Chris. He wants the house to come alive again and I must say it's really quiet with just the two of us upstairs and Mrs Garside and Joyce pottering about downstairs in the kitchen.

Laura smiled at Polly's antics as she danced around the kitchen, remembering it was something she used to do as a child.

"What's all the racket?" George said as he ambled down the stairs and Laura laughed as she told him what Polly had suggested".

"Go and have Christmas at the big house, eh? Well, that's a turn up. Never thought we'd be mixing with the posh folk."

Polly turned around in shock, her face telling its own story as she looked from George to Laura and back to see whether he meant it or not. There was no smile on George's face and Laura had gone white. "You can't mean that, George," Polly said.

"I was joking. Just look at you two. Anybody would think you'd seen a ghost." He smiled then and hugged them close and Polly relaxed at his words. Laura though pulled out of his arms, "That was a terrible thing to say, George, even as a joke. You know Chris and Polly aren't like that."

"I know, and I'm sorry. We'll come for Christmas. Just wait till Emma finds out. She'll be swanking in front of her mates."

"I hope not. We'll never hear the end of it if she does. Folks around here don't like it if someone is different and we've got to come back, don't forget."

"Yes, I know. Not for long though I hope. I've heard there's plans for a new council estate on the fields at the bottom of Ramsden Avenue and I'm going to put our names down as soon as I can. I'm fed up of having to go down to that awful lavatory block out the back. It's like living in the dark ages round here."

"I can't wait," Laura answered having recovered her good humour. "It'll be lovely to have our own lav and wash house again instead of having to share it with six other families."

"At least you won't have to think about that over Christmas. You can have a choice of bathrooms, so there," Polly countered. "So if that's not posh I don't know what is."

The tension was eased and they were all laughing together when Emma came running in.

"Mam, can we go and get my new wellies now? You said we could ages ago."

Laura looked a little embarrassed in front of Polly, but her sister's attention was all on Emma now.

"Oh, Aunty Polly," she gasped. "You hug so tight I can't breathe."

"I know, but I love you that much, I could eat you up," she laughed.

Laura went to get her coat from the cupboard under the stairs and put on her own well-worn boots. She went into the living room to get her purse and checked that there was enough money in it to buy the wellingtons for Emma. It was just as well they didn't have to buy Christmas dinner now that they were going to stay with Polly and Chris or there wouldn't have been enough. Smiling, she went through to the kitchen to find Emma telling Polly what Father Christmas was going to bring her. The list consisted of a toy sweet shop and a doll she had seen in Dewey's shop, together with an apple, an orange and some monkey nuts in her stocking.

"You will be a lucky girl if you get those then, won't you?" Polly remarked looking up at George who turned away, but not before Polly had caught a glimpse of despair in his eyes.

"Come on then, let's be off to see what Miss Mather has got in the latest fashion of wellington boots." Laura laughed and went to kiss George before she left. Polly took hold of Emma's hand and walked out of the back door, leaving Laura and George to have a quiet word before they set off.

The crisp winter air was just what Laura needed to blow away the last vestiges of depression which had threatened to settle on her shoulders. The walk up Fleetgate to the Miss Mather's shoe shop took them about ten minutes. They passed the small-windowed Victorian shops and Polly was again struck by how little the town had changed. Mr Lacey could be seen behind his counter selling groceries and Grasbys tobacconist and newspaper shop was exactly as she remembered it. Polly turned on the threshold of Miss Mathers shoe shop and looked at Laura.

"I haven't been in this shop for years, Laura. Does she still chuck everything into a heap in the middle of the room?"

Laura laughed, "Yes, how she finds anything I don't know. I think she opens the boxes and just tips them out. They're tied up with string into pairs but looking for sizes can take her ages."

They entered to the sound of a tinkling bell and the smell of leather, and Polly recognised the small counter which ran the width of the room with Miss Mather sat in her usual place behind the cash register. At the back of the shop but in view of the customers, was an old man stooping over a last and banging segs into a boot.

"Hello, Miss Mather. I'd like a pair of wellington boots for Emma please." Laura looked the middle-aged woman in the eye, trying not to laugh at the heap of black rubberised boots behind her. Polly too tried to keep her giggles under control but each gave a wry smile when the older woman got up and ambled over to the pile.

"What size is she?"

"Thirteen I think. But she'll probably need thick socks under them so maybe a one would be better."

Miraculously she pulled a pair of boots from the pile which were indeed a size one and handed them over the counter to Laura who sat Emma on a chair to try them on. They were a bit roomy but Laura thought they would last her longer, so after Emma had plodded up and down the shop a couple of times she decided to buy them. It was then Polly noticed Laura's own boots had seen better days and pointed to a pair of dark brown, fur-lined ankle boots in the window. There was nothing stylish about them but they did look warm and practical.

"What do you think of these, Laura?" she pointed to the boots in question.

"Very nice, but a bit pricey for me," Laura replied.

"Why don't you try them on and see what they feel like?"

Laura looked doubtful. "Oh, alright, I take a size six. I'm just trying them on mind. George would kill me if I went back with these."

Miss Mather reached behind her and took a box from one of the shelves. These at least weren't consigned to the heap in the middle of the floor. Laura sat on the chair recently vacated by Emma and pulled the boots on. Polly noticed that she had no socks or stockings on and her feet were covered in angry looking chilblains.

"The fur is lovely and warm, Polly. But like I said, I can't afford them."

"Have them anyway - as a Christmas present from me and Chris."

Laura looked knowingly at Polly and smiled. "I knew there'd be a catch somewhere. No, Polly, it's really kind of you but I couldn't possibly take them. They're five bob and that's a lot of money for a pair of boots."

"If you don't take them, I'll buy them anyway and you'll get them on Christmas day, so there."

"Yes, Mam, go on have them for Christmas. They'll keep your feet lovely and warm".

Polly watched as Laura looked into the excited face of her daughter and knew she couldn't disappoint her even though George might have something to say when she got home.

"Alright then, thanks. It's really good of you."

Polly smiled as she handed over the money to Miss Mather and the wellington boots were paid for out of Laura's purse. Both packages were wrapped in brown paper and tied with string and the little bell tinkled again as they left the shop.

"I don't know what George will say when he sees these," Laura pointed to the bigger package containing her boots.

"If you want to, I'll take them and wrap them up for you to open on Christmas day. He can't get angry then can he?"

"I think it might be better if you do, Polly. I don't want to make him feel any worse about not working than he already does."

With this decided they parted company, Laura to return home, and Polly to do a bit of shopping in the Market Place. "Don't forget to tell Emma about Christmas," she said to Laura before moving on.

Half a minute later she turned around to find Emma running up behind her. Breathless, the little girl flung her arms around Polly's waist and hugged her tight. "Oh, Aunt Polly, thank you for inviting us for Christmas. Won't it be lovely? I can't wait to come and sleep at your house."

Polly hugged her in return and whispered that Father Christmas would be coming to The Elms too, but she must be a good girl for her mam and dad. Emma turned around and ran back to her mother who laughed and waved goodbye to her sister.

***

Walking back to The Elms, Polly was deep in thought regarding George's initial response to the invitation to spend Christmas with her and Chris. Did he really think they were different? She resolved to make less of her good fortune in marrying Chris and to make sure she didn't inadvertently offend George in some way. It would be difficult though, seeing her sister go without

26

when she herself had so much and would willingly share it with her. She crossed the road onto Winship Flags and made her way up to Hungate, where she came across her old friend, Mary Simpson, whom she knew from her school days. Mary's father still owned the bakery on the corner of King Street and Polly was happy to hear that the family were still well.

"Why don't you come back to the house with me?" Polly asked. "We can have a good old natter."

Mary looked downcast, "I'm sorry, Polly. I can't at the moment. My husband has taken my little boy out to see his mother for a couple of hours while I do some shopping and housework." She saw Polly's disappointment and added, "But I'd love to come in the week sometime after Christmas."

Polly immediately issued an invitation for them to attend the planned New Year party. Mary replied that she would ask her husband if they could come. As Polly continued on her way she realised that her life was quite empty apart from Chris. Her desire for a family was eating her up inside and she decided to speak to her husband about seeing a doctor after the Christmas holiday.

***

Arriving back at The Elms, Polly walked into the living room and saw Chris sitting in front of the fire warming his toes with The Times newspaper discarded in a messy heap beside him. He was just about to take the first bite from a freshly baked batch of scones and she laughed as he coughed when a crumb went down the wrong way. She patted his back but he continued to cough and splutter until she handed him his tea and he recovered himself a little.

"That serves you right for sitting here doing nothing while I've been out shopping in the cold," she said and ducked as a cushion came flying her way. She caught it with ease and threw it back with surprising force, making Chris laugh out loud.

"I'll have you know I've been thinking higher thoughts and trying to decide what I'm going to do with myself now I'm in Civvy Street."

"And what did you decide?"

"I didn't – maybe I'll send you to work and live off your earnings," he smiled mischievously.

"We'd starve within a fortnight!" Polly laughed.

"No, seriously," Chris continued, "I thought about politics or business and maybe even teaching. What do you think?"

"I think you should take more time to think about it after Christmas."

"Maybe you're right, but I can't sit here idle for months on end. Canada really opened my eyes to the opportunities my education might have to offer."

"Yes, well privately educated young men are always in demand."

Mrs Garside walked in at that moment with more tea and scones.

"I thought I heard you, Polly. I've just made these and thought you might like some."

"Thanks, Mrs Garside. They do look tempting." She placed a scone on her plate and poured a cup of tea from the bone china teapot. "By the way – I've asked Laura, George and Emma to come and have Christmas with us and they've agreed," she grinned happily. "Why don't you come and stay, Mrs Garside, we've got plenty of room. Me and Laura will help with the cooking as Joyce won't be there on Christmas day."

"I suppose I might as well, I'll be in the kitchen anyway. Are you sure you don't mind?"

"We've more rooms than we can fill and we don't expect you to work all the time. You'd be more than welcome to join us."

"That's very kind, Polly. I'd be happy to accept. I would probably have a nap in the afternoon though and listen to the radio."

"Good. It'll be lovely to have a house full of people at Christmas, won't it Chris?"

"Definitely! Martin says he might be back by then too," he answered through a mouthful of crumbs.

"That's wonderful news? When did you find out?" Polly was delighted to hear that Chris's older brother, Martin, would be joining them. She hadn't seen him since her wedding day."

"He rang earlier while you were out, and that's not all – he's bringing a young lady he's met in France. Antoinette her name is, but she speaks fluent English thankfully, so we don't have to worry about the language barrier."

"It gets better and better." Polly's eyes were shining with excitement and Chris was relieved. He had been worried about her recently but planning the Christmas festivities seemed to be putting the colour back into her cheeks. "This is going to be the best Christmas ever."

THREE

In the days leading up to Christmas, The Elms saw another explosion of activity as bedrooms were cleaned thoroughly once again, beds were made up, and trimmings festooned the downstairs rooms. The entrance hall was decked with holly and mistletoe and paper chains hung from the ceiling. It was a large house with three floors and enough bedrooms to accommodate many more guests than had been invited.

Mrs Garside had opted for a room on the first floor near the back of the house so that it was as quiet as possible, and Emma had chosen a bedroom for her parents with a small dressing room leading from it which contained a single bed just for her. She was so excited to be in such a grand house and her little eyes sparkled and danced with each new discovery as she explored the other rooms. Her greatest find was a door which led down from the upstairs landing to the kitchen. She called it a secret passage but Polly told her that when she had worked there as a nursery maid she had had to use the stairs all the time, as did the other domestic staff.

Polly was on cloud nine as Laura, George, and Emma brought their cases into their temporary bedrooms and made themselves at home.

"Come down when you're ready, Laura, and we'll have a cuppa. I think Chris has something stronger in mind for George if he's up for it."

"I'm never backwards in coming forwards if there's a tipple on offer," George remarked, winking at Polly. She moved towards him and gave him a hug.

"I'm so glad to have you here – all of you."

"It's good of you to invite us. We should have a merry old time shouldn't we, Emma?"

George ruffled Emma's hair and she giggled excitedly. "I can't wait for Father Christmas to come, Aunty Polly. He will know I'm here, won't he?" she asked seriously.

"I've already written a note to him and he knows where to find you, so don't worry. You can leave him a mince pie and a glass of whisky on the kitchen table if you want to."

Polly closed the bedroom door and smiled. She was so pleased to have them that she knew she wouldn't want them to leave when the time came. She could hear Emma running from her room back to her parents' room and prayed inwardly that she would soon have a family of her own to fill the big house. Sir Giles and Lady Beauchamp were staying in Canada for a while longer but when they did come back they had offered to make a wing of the house over to Chris and Polly so that they might call it their own. It was a generous offer and Polly was making plans already. Lady Beauchamp had hinted that there could be some structural alterations too to give them more privacy which was welcomed by both Chris and Polly.

Downstairs in the living room the Christmas tree sparkled with baubles and tinsel which had been brought up from the depths of the basement where it had been stored for years. The tree had been ordered from Dewey's shop and was one of the last in the consignment of real trees which were still scarce. It was planted in a huge tub which had been used for years in the Beauchamp household and now that it was decorated it looked a picture. The scent of pine hung in the air and the only thing that was missing was a fairy on the top. Polly had deliberately left this item off so that Emma could place it there herself. The furniture too had been rediscovered under dust sheets and dragged back up the stairs to sit once more in its former position, polished and shining as if it had always been there. Polly and Chris reminisced on the time when it had been stored just after the war started, and Lady Beauchamp and little Michael, Chris's younger half-brother, had flown off to Canada to stay with relatives for the duration.

Polly went down to the kitchen to find Mrs Garside. She was sitting in her favourite chair by the range cooker with her feet up on a stool. She snored softly as Polly tiptoed round her to fill the kettle at the large Belfast sink. The sound of crockery being placed on a tray brought her out of her nap and on seeing Polly she immediately jumped up to start helping.

"No, Mrs Garside. I insist you let me do this. There'll be plenty for you to do later when the house gets even fuller. Martin and Antoinette will be here soon. They're getting a taxi from the station. It'll be lovely to see him again, won't it?"

"It will. I never really took to him when he was growing up, but after he saved your life during the war and we found out he was really working for the Intelligence, then I thought very differently of him."

"He played his part well, didn't he? I really despised him for a long time and he frightened me. Little did I know he was chasing spies and working to protect us all from that Jane woman who we all hated."

"Well, she got her come-uppance didn't she?" Mrs Garside laughed.

"She certainly did. Now then, what can I put on this tray? Shall we have one of your delicious buns?" Polly said, changing the subject.

"You can, Polly, but don't forget there's still rationing and I haven't got many coupons left."

"Laura has brought hers and we have a few left. If we need anything else it will have to wait until the shops open again."

"I'll need them for the new year party if you want to put a spread on."

"Alright, we'll talk about it after Christmas, shall we?"

Polly put half a dozen buns onto a plate and poured hot water into the teapot. She added a jug of milk but left the sugar bowl off the tray. Nearly everybody had their tea without sugar these days as there had been so little available during the war they had become used to it. The tray was heavy but she managed to stagger up the stairs without spilling anything and took it into the living room. Laura and George were watching Emma as she sat on Chris's knee and listened to a story. They looked a little uncomfortable, like fish out of water, but Polly ushered them into chairs and put the tray down on a small table. "You pour our Laura. Emma, do you want to put the fairy at the top of the tree?"

"Yes please, Aunty Polly." Emma's eyes shone as she scuttled off Chris's lap. George lifted her up high so that she could reach with the fairy and everyone clapped as they watched.

Once Emma had returned to her mother, Polly noticed George was standing awkwardly again.

"Chris, are you going to get George a whisky or something?"

34

"Of course, what would you like, George? There's quite a variety in the cabinet over there. What's your poison?" George followed him over to the drinks cabinet and looked through the contents.

"Crikey, Chris. You've more bottles and glasses here than behind the bar at The Sloop."

"There's some beer down in the kitchen keeping cold, if you would rather have that?" Chris offered.

"No, I'm just gob-smacked at how much you've got here."

"It's all been stored downstairs in the cellar whilst we've been away. It should be alright though. I was going to try some out of each of the open bottles but Polly wouldn't let me. She said if I did, she would make me throw it away!" he laughed.

"He's not joking either," Polly said, "but I told him he'd be spending Christmas in hospital if he tried that."

George chose a whisky and soda and Chris joined him. The glasses had been newly washed and the cut glass sparkled in the light from the fire. It was just the kind of Christmas Eve Polly had dreamed of all the time she had been away. Chris put the wireless on and they listened to Benny Goodman and his Orchestra playing some swing music. Polly loved Jimmy Dorsey and Glenn Miller and thought of the days at the Assembly Rooms when they would dance the night away. Polly cuddled Emma for a while before Laura decided it was time for her to go to bed. After a few protests Emma knew she was beaten and Laura took her to bed but not before Polly remembered her promise that Emma could put a mince pie and a drink out for Santa.

They went down to the kitchen with a bottle of whisky and Mrs Garside provided the pies while Laura poured the whisky into the glasses. "Is one of these for Rudolph, Mam?" Emma asked innocently.

"Yes, poor old Rudolph has a very busy night ahead too, doesn't he?"

Satisfied that Father Christmas would have something to warm him up Emma went to bed with assurances that he would not forget she had moved house for a while.

It was while Laura was putting Emma to bed that they heard a commotion in the hallway. Chris went to investigate and Polly realised from the laughs and exchanges that Martin had arrived with his lady friend. Polly couldn't resist the temptation to go and see what she looked like so she followed Chris into the hall.

"Polly!" shouted Martin. "Let me look at you. My, you've grown up since I last saw you, and more beautiful than ever. Come here and give me a hug. It's been so long."

"Hello, Martin. It's good to see you too, and still as handsome," she countered, and looked over his shoulder at Antoinette who stood with a suitcase clutched in her hand. "This must be Antoinette." Polly left Martin's embrace and smiled. She moved towards the young woman and reached out to shake the young woman's hand. Without a second glance she promptly handed over her suitcase and walked towards Chris.

Martin quickly took the suitcase from Polly's grip. "I'll take that and put it upstairs. Which rooms are we to have, Polly?" His attempt to cover up for his friend's actions weren't lost on Polly and she tried to answer in kind.

"I've made up your bed in your old room and Antoinette is along the corridor. You'll see when you get up there. George and Laura are staying too but

36

they're on the opposite side to you so that Emma isn't disturbed."

"Righto. Come on, Toni," he guided Antoinette, who was hanging on to Chris's hand, towards the stairs. "Let's get settled in and then we'll join you."

Polly rejoined George in the living room and Chris came in a few seconds later.

"Did you see what she did, Chris?" Polly was indignant.

"No, what did she do?"

"I went to shake her hand and she gave me her suitcase instead and made a bee-line for you."

"Well, I suppose she didn't realise. Maybe she's tired.

"I think Martin might have trouble with that one." Polly was not happy that Chris had shrugged off her complaint so easily. She silently fumed until Laura came back into the room, having managed to get Emma to sleep at last.

"She's so excited about Father Christmas coming tomorrow she couldn't settle. Was that Martin I heard come in?"

"Yes, he and Antoinette are just getting settled and then they'll be down," Chris answered.

"What's she like?" Laura looked at Polly but she just raised one eyebrow and muttered, "Ask Chris."

Laura glanced at Chris who shrugged his shoulders and an uneasy silence fell. George picked up a newspaper and hid behind it while Laura tried to make desultory conversation until at last, Martin, minus Antoinette, entered the room. He shook hands with George and kissed Laura's cheek before going to the cabinet and helping himself to a drink. Polly was amazed when he knocked back a neat whisky before re-filling his glass and settling himself on the sofa.

"Is everything alright, Martin? Where's Antoinette?" she asked, noting the change in his demeanour.

"She's upstairs getting changed. I'm sorry about earlier, Polly. She's so used to servants hanging around her that she expects everyone to be at her beck and call. I've just put her straight though."

"Well, let's forget it then shall we? I'll go down and make some sandwiches for us. Mrs Garside is a bit tired so we won't bother with a meal tonight, but we'll have a good breakfast in the morning."

"Thanks, Polly. Fancy old Mrs Garside still being here. I'll come down with you and say hello."

A couple of hours later and sandwiches had been devoured and drinks had flowed liberally. Antoinette still hadn't put in an appearance, so it was obvious that she was still sulking in her room. It had been a pleasant evening but both Polly and Laura were tired, so after washing the dishes and leaving the kitchen ready for the morning, they went to bed.

The last thing Chris and Martin did was to put a hastily scribbled thank you note next to the mince pie plate and gulp down the whisky. Emma would be pleased to know that her offering had been gratefully received.

**

George and Laura were woken at six o'clock by a cry of delight from Emma who bounded into their room holding a stocking in her little hands. She jumped onto the bed and snuggled in between her parents, their

38

bleary eyed reception lost on the child. "He's been, Mam. Father Christmas has been and left me a stocking." She opened up the top and looked into the depths, which was in fact one of George's long socks, and began to explore the contents. The delight in her eyes as she pulled out an orange and then an apple was undimmed until at last she had taken everything out and laid them in front of her. "Look, Mam and Dad, there's nuts too. Oooh, aren't I lucky to have all this?" She looked around for confirmation as her mother and father nodded their agreement. "I'll share it though," Emma added seriously, "I want you to have some of it too."

George swallowed a lump in his throat as he watched his beloved daughter's delight in the meagre contents of the sock. How he wished he could give her more. She was such a sweet child and deserved a father who could work and earn money to keep her properly fed and clothed. He looked around the room at the comfort it offered and thought of their own sparse bedroom back home. He thought of the draughts from ill-fitting windows and doors and tried to stifle the resentment he felt that Chris and Polly had all this. He knew he was being unreasonable. Polly would share her last breath with them and Chris was as amenable and charitable as anyone could be. The word 'charitable' stuck in his throat. He would resist being a charity case and work for his keep. His mind was filled with things he could do around the place to make up for the comfort and food he was being given. He had felt better for the last week so he imagined himself chopping wood and bringing in coal.

"Come on, George. Let's get up and see if anyone else is around. We can have a cuppa in the kitchen where it's cosy," she said, obviously trying to jolly him out of his gathering depression.

"Yes let's, Dad," Emma joined in, and leapt on youthful legs onto the bedside rug. "Oooh, this rug is lovely and warm," she announced innocently.

George thought of the cold lino in Emma's room at home but bit off the retort that sprang to his lips. It wasn't the child's fault. She didn't see things like a grown-up would, but he got out of bed and grabbed his threadbare dressing gown with as much grace as he could muster.

Downstairs in the kitchen the range was lit and ready to accept the chicken and a piece of beef that Polly and Laura had had to queue for hours to get. Laura's mouth watered just thinking about it. The surprise was the huge breakfast which was put in front of them. The sausage and egg was accompanied by fried bread and black pudding with mushrooms on the side. A large hamper had arrived from Canada earlier in the week, sent by Sir Giles and Lady Beauchamp who had read of the shortage of food and had supplied many luxury treats not seen in England since well before the war. Mrs Garside had squirreled it away to surprise everyone and showed Laura the ham that was hung in the larder waiting to be cooked.

Forgetting about the previous evening, Laura watched as Emma looked around the room.

"What's the matter, Emma? Have you lost something?"

"I was just looking to see if Father Christmas had eaten his mince pies and drunk his whisky."

Mrs Garside winked at Laura and produced the plate and glasses. "It looks like he did, Emma, and he's left a note for you – look."

Emma squealed in delight as she took the note which had been left for her and held it to her heart. "Look, Mam. I've got a note from Father Christmas and he says he liked the mince pies. He says Rudolph says thank you as well."

"Well, aren't you just the luckiest girl to get a note from Father Christmas?"

Emma nodded happily and went running up to the living room in search of Polly but returned almost immediately having found the room empty.

George leaned back in his seat replete from the cooked breakfast and the toast which had followed. Laura noted how much healthier he looked after just a day of good food and relaxation and wished things could be like this all the time. "I'm going to get dressed now and see to what needs to be done." He looked at Mrs Garside, "Do you want some coal and logs bringing in?" he asked.

"Yes please, George. The fires will need making up in the living room and the dining room today."

"I'll get to it then."

Laura watched with some concern as he pushed back his seat and left the room via the back stairs.

Emma was too excited to notice what her father was doing and fidgeted impatiently waiting for Polly and Chris to come downstairs. "Shall I go and wake them up, Mam?"

"No, don't you dare. Let them sleep a bit longer. It's only seven o'clock."

"Mrs Garside is up," Emma pouted.

There was a noise and a dishevelled Antoinette accompanied by Martin, made their way down the main stairs. Laura stood up to welcome them both, "Good morning, I'm Polly's sister, Laura, are you feeling better this morning?"

"Yes. But hungry." The reply was curt but Laura refused to let some foreigner spoil her Christmas and turned her attention to Martin. "Mrs Garside has excelled herself so I hope you're hungry too."

"I could eat a horse," was the reply, so Laura took Emma, who had turned shy in front of the newcomers, and led her up the back stairs to get washed and dressed, leaving the couple to have their breakfast.

By ten o'clock everyone was gathered in the living room and Polly could see Emma's impatience as she cast frequent glances at the parcels under the tree. Laura kept a restraining hand on Emma but in the end the little girl could stand it no longer.

"Mam, can I have a look at the parcels, please?"

"Not yet, love. You'll have to wait a bit."

Polly was just as eager to give Emma her presents but, as hostess, knew she would have to make certain all her guests were comfortable first. "Shall we have coffee and mince pies before church?" she asked. Everyone agreed it was a good idea but Emma's groan was audible and frustrated tears threatened to gather. Polly knelt down and whispered in her ear that she could open one present before church and then open the rest when she got back.

"Oh, thank you, Aunty Polly. They all look so lovely under the tree. I just wanted to look at them a bit closer."

Taking her hand, Polly led her to the tree where she found a flat parcel wrapped in colourful paper. Emma looked towards her mother and father, eyes shining with excitement and ran back to them holding her present aloft.

Laura sat with her on the sofa and all eyes watched as Emma peeled the paper off. "Oh look, Mam, it's a book called *Alice in Wonderland*. Isn't it lovely?"

It was indeed lovely. The hard cover was emblazoned with the title "*Alice in Wonderland*" by Lewis Carroll, and had drawings of The Mad Hatter's Tea Party on the front and The White Rabbit jumping into a hole on the back. The illustrations inside were of exquisite quality and seemed almost too good for a child.

Emma looked up with a serious face, "I promise I'll really look after it, Aunty Polly." Even Antoinette seemed enchanted by the little girl's promise.

Everyone including Mrs Garside made their way down Whitecross Street and crossed the road to St. Mary's Church where Polly and Chris had been married almost six years previously. The church bells were ringing out in celebration of the birth of the Saviour and the pews were packed with people, some of whom Polly hadn't seen for years. She waved at a few faces she recognised and felt such a sense of peace inside her that she grabbed Chris's hand to steady herself. "Are you alright, Polly?" his concern written on his face.

"Yes, I really am," she answered confidently and her smile was genuine.

Chris looked at her radiant face and fell in love all over again. Not that there was ever a time he didn't love her, but today he wanted her to have everything he could give her, and that included children. As he fell to his knees to pray before the service began, he asked for a child for Polly. Surely, God would grant his request on this day if no other.

***

As soon as they arrived back at the house, George changed into some old clothes, rolled up his sleeves and went outside to chop some wood and fill up the coal scuttles, his earlier efforts having been used up in no time. The wood shed was next to the coal house and all was quiet except for the sound of the axe as he chopped away at the logs. He had stacked the chopped wood neatly in the shed and then started to shovel coal when he thought he heard someone or something shuffling around in the woodshed. He stood for a moment, ears straining to hear any further movement, but there was nothing. Chris and Martin joined him with empty coal scuttles and as he shovelled, they took away the full ones. It was just as he had closed and locked the coal house door that he heard the noise again. This time he was sure he had heard something and dashed around to the log shed just in time to see someone disappear behind a wicker screen separating the logs from the chopped wood.

"Come out, whoever you are." George shouted but nothing moved. Chris had heard the shout and ran to where George was standing.

"There's someone hiding in there." George pointed to the wicker screen.

"Are you sure? It could be a rat or a mouse."

"I saw someone. I know I did." The perspiration caused by his efforts to chop the wood and shovel the coal was drying on his skin and he began to shiver.

Chris obviously saw that George wasn't up to tussling with anyone and said, "I'll go in and see who's there. If he makes a break for it let him go. He probably won't come back."

The words, although he knew were meant kindly, riled George even more, "I can handle it - I'm not an invalid you know."

"No, no, that's not what I meant. Just be careful that's all."

At that moment they heard the logs slide again and saw a figure move, "Please, I mean no harm. I am prisoner of war. I should be with my friends."

The German accent wasn't lost on George. "Come on out then - let's have a look at you."

The man emerged slowly from behind the screen with his hands in the air. He looked to be in his early twenties with a sparse golden beard springing from an otherwise smooth chin. He was tall with broad shoulders and a slim waist. George noticed his hands were large and calloused.

"What's your name?" Chris approached the young man and indicated he should put his arms down.

"I am Kurt von Haussen and I became lost yesterday. I hide in your wood shed but I am very cold."

"You'd better come in and tell us about yourself." Chris indicated the way into the house and George followed.

Inside the kitchen they found Martin putting the kettle on. He turned around and gasped in surprise at the stranger in their midst.

"Well! Who have we here then?" he asked good-naturedly.

"I am Kurt, Sir. I am lost here."

"Well, Kurt – sit yourself down and have a drink. You must be frozen."

When they were all sat around the kitchen table with steaming coffee cups, Kurt began his story.

45

"Have you heard of the German Workshop Company?"

"I have," answered George, "but I thought they were based in Italy."

"Yes, I was with them in Italy until August 1945, and then we were supposed to be sent back to our homes in Germany."

"I was out in Italy in 1940," said George but I came back in 1941 then got sent to Burma."

"Then I feel sorry for you. I heard of terrible times out there."

"It was no picnic I can tell you. Anyway, carry on with your story."

"Well, some of us were sent to Liverpool and some to other places. I was sent to Brigg where I helped with harvest and have been there ever since, working the land with other prisoners. Yesterday, some of us were sent to an unexploded bomb which had been found on the river bank."

"Isn't that against the Geneva Convention?" Martin asked.

"Yes, but we don't complain. We are treated well and have adequate food and shelter. We just want to go home."

His voice wobbled with emotion and his eyes filled with unshed tears showing his youth and vulnerability. Even George was moved by his story. He knew the deep desire to be home among family and friends instead of being forced to stay in a foreign country which sapped your strength and left you a shadow of your former self.

"I was sent further down the bank to look for more bombs and when the truck came to take us back to camp I missed it. They probably looked for me but I was lost and eventually found myself wandering your streets in the dark. I saw lights on in this house and found the wood shed. It was dry so I stayed there till you found me just now."

"You're lucky the weather has been a bit milder lately," Martin said. "Unfortunately, we can't do anything for you today as its Christmas Day, but I might be able to put a call through to the camp commandant to let him know you're here. They can pick you up tomorrow perhaps. Would you like to join us for Christmas dinner?" he offered.

The young man's eyes opened wide, "Oh, yes please. I would love to have dinner with you."

"I think you could do with a bath first, and I'll find you some clean clothes. Come on, I'll take you and introduce you to the ladies."

All eyes turned in their direction as the four men entered the living room. The stranger looked the worse for wear and Polly immediately went to him.

"You poor thing, you look frozen," she said sympathetically, taking in his dishevelled appearance.

"I am better now thank you, madam. I have had coffee to warm me."

"This is Kurt, Polly. He's a German prisoner of war from the camp in Brigg. He got lost yesterday so has stayed in our wood shed overnight. We've invited him to stay for dinner."

This last piece of information brought a gasp from Mrs Garside and Antoinette protested. "You give food to this man?" Antoinette asked.

"Yes, we do," Polly answered quickly. "The war's over now and he's just a young man who needs help."

"We do not do things like that in France."

"I'm sure you do, Antoinette. I'm sure if it was your brother in a foreign land who needed help you would hope someone would offer him refuge and a meal, especially at Christmas."

Antoinette looked suitably chastised and returned to looking at Emma's presents with her.

"I'm going to run him a bath, Polly," Martin said and I'll give him some of my clothes to change into for the time being."

Polly smiled at Kurt who moved to take her hand. "I am grateful, madam, for your hospitality. Thank you."

FOUR

After the presents had been opened and declared to be 'just what I needed', Mrs Garside announced that dinner would be served in the dining room. Antoinette said very little and spent most of her time with Emma. She sat with her, looking through her books and listening to her stories about school, and her friends. She raised an eyebrow when Mrs Garside joined them for dinner at the dining table, commenting, "We don't usually allow servants to eat with us,"

Polly gritted her teeth and replied, "Mrs Garside is not a servant, she has been part of this family for years," which elicited a Gallic shrug but no further comment.

Kurt looked a little uncomfortable as he sat in silence. The beef and chicken was accompanied by sprouts, cabbage, peas and carrots. It was mouth-wateringly delicious though and he ate his fill with gratitude. He answered questions and offered bits of information about his family. "I am worried that they have nowhere to live now. The winters can be very cold, but I am sure they will have gone to my aunt's house in the Black Forest. It is beautiful there."

***

George endured the day as best he could. He ate the food put in front of him and joined in the conversation when it was directed his way. He envied the ease with which Chris and Martin carried on as if there had been no war. They seemed to take it all for granted, the decorous dining room, the elegant furnishings and the heat from the fires. The heating from the radiators acted as a back-up, making sure that the whole house was warm. This was a revelation to George who had only known coal fires. They even drank wine with their Christmas dinner. He had only ever tasted wine in Italy when he was with the army, and that was only because the water supply wasn't much good. Although the food was excellent and Polly and Laura had helped to cook it, it turned to ashes in his mouth as he thought of how little he had contributed. He and Laura went without so that Emma could have clothes, but even this didn't help. Laura deserved better than he could give her and it was Laura herself who provided for the family by working part-time. He was just a burden and he knew it. The boots that Polly and Chris had bought for Laura rankled. He knew she needed them and deserved them, and felt a failure for not being able to provide them himself. He had accepted the new warm, quilted dressing gown with a smile but vowed he wouldn't wear it when he got home. It would hang behind the bedroom door on a hook gathering dust if he got his way, and the accompanying slippers would sit at the bottom of the wardrobe. He wouldn't accept their charity. A man had to have his pride.

"George, are you listening?" Laura was nudging his arm. "Martin is asking if you want a brandy with your coffee"

"Oh, er, yes .... thanks. I was miles away."

"I think we should have a toast to the ladies who cooked our wonderful dinner. What do you say Chris?" Martin raised his glass and smiled around the table.

"I should say so. First class food ladies, and thank you." Chris raised his glass too, as did George and

Kurt, and Polly and Laura giggled and nudged Mrs Garside, who was looking sleepy, but Antoinette remained silent and withdrawn.

"Let's clear away then." Polly stood up and Laura began to pick up the plates.

"No. Please. Let me do this for you. You have been so kind I want to help." Kurt stood up and motioned that the ladies should sit down.

"Well, if you insist. Thank you," Polly responded, glad not to have to face the mountain of dishes in the kitchen.

"Looks like we'll have to do our bit as well, Chris, we can't leave it to Kurt here to do the honours. What would he think of us?" Martin said.

"All men to the kitchen," Chris ordered, and laughed as the men stood to attention and saluted, joining in the fun. George led the way with dishes piled high.

While the men were away, Mrs Garside decided to go up to her room and have a nap and Emma, exhausted from a combination of present opening, dinner and excitement, put her head on a cushion and went to sleep in a chair. Polly drew the curtains and the glow from the fire and a standard lamp in one corner and the brightly decorated tree in another, made a cosy picture. Antoinette was leafing through a magazine when Polly asked, "Tell us about yourself, Antoinette. How did you meet Martin?"

She looked a little surprised to have been asked, "We met during the war when the Resistance were hiding British airmen. He was my contact."

Laura looked shocked, "You mean you were in the Resistance?"

"Yes, my father was the Comte de Valois. We are an old family, you understand. My father was killed by the Nazis because he would not co-operate with them and he would not order the village to co-operate either. They shot him as an example to all the other men."

"No! That's terrible. You poor thing, no wonder you didn't like Kurt."

"I realise that not all Germans are Nazis, and Kurt seems a nice young man, but I don't trust people easily. I have been betrayed too many times."

Polly found a new respect for their guest and urged further confidences from her. "What has happened to your mother?" Polly asked tentatively.

"She was taken away by the SS to work in Germany. We don't know yet if she has survived."

"And your home, will you be able to go back to it?"

"That is why I am here. There is some trouble with my inheritance. Martin is going to try and help me. It all depends on whether we can find my mother."

"Shouldn't you be looking in Germany then?" Polly asked, puzzled.

"Things in Germany are not good at this time. I have heard through various people that my mother escaped to England and has been in hiding. I am here to search for her too."

"I wish you luck with that then. Are you going to London?"

"Yes, we will be leaving the day after tomorrow."
Polly reached over and squeezed Antoinette's hand. She realised she had judged this young woman too harshly. Life had dealt her a dangerous and deadly hand, so there was no wonder she was often silent and withdrawn. "I hope you find your mother," she said quietly.

"Merci. But I hear from Martin that your war was not uneventful. I believe you were wounded by a German spy."

"Yes, that's right. I try not to wear anything that will show the scar, so sleeveless summer dresses are out for me." Polly laughed, trying to keep her voice low in case Emma woke up and overheard.

When the men came back fresh from the kitchen they put the radio on and moved the furniture back to give them room to dance. Emma woke up and was overjoyed to see her father and mother laughing together. There had been precious few moments of gaiety in the last few months, so when her mother flopped in a chair breathless, George reached down and picked Emma up from the chair and danced around the room with her, bringing forth squeals of delight. Unfortunately, the unaccustomed exertion was short-lived and George put Emma down quickly when he felt pains in his chest. Laura's attention was elsewhere when he sat down gasping for breath. She turned quickly in his direction just in time to see the colour drain from his face and his lips turn blue.

"George! What's the matter? Are you alright?" The terror in her voice alerted Polly as she danced with Chris and the music stopped abruptly.

"Quick, Chris. Bring George a brandy or something. He's not very well."

Slowly, the colour began to seep back into George's face as he sipped the drink and he became aware of people staring at him. "I'm alright," he snapped. "Go back to your dancing. Don't bother about me. I'll be fine".

"We're just a bit bothered about you, old man," Chris said, putting one hand on his shoulder.

"Old man's right, isn't it? That's all I am – an old man. Useless, can't even dance with my daughter without nearly passing out. I'm off to bed. Sorry if I've spoilt your fun."

"I didn't mean....." Chris began but George was through the door, slamming it behind him.

"Let him go, Chris. He'll be alright. I'll go up and see him in a few minutes." Laura looked at Polly and shook her head.

Emma's bottom lip was quivering and Laura pulled her onto her lap and hugged her for a few seconds before saying, "Don't worry, love. Daddy will be fine. He's just tired that's all. I'll take you up to bed in a bit, and you can see for yourself. I know – shall we play snap?"

Emma's eyes lit up and she wiped her eyes, "Yes please, Mam."

The party atmosphere was never recovered so after Emma was taken to bed and Laura declared that she could do with an early night, the four remaining young people played cards, talked and reminisced until the small hours.

Laura woke in the night to find George up and staring out of the window.

"Are you alright, George? Are you feeling better?" she whispered, so as not to wake Emma in the adjoining room.

George turned and walked back to the bed. "I'm a lot better. Go back to sleep."

"I can't if I know you're pacing the floor. What's the matter? You've been really mardy ever since we came here. And don't say there's nothing wrong, because I know better. Come on. Let's go down and get a drink. We'll wake Emma up if we talk up here."

They put on their dressing gowns – Laura insisting he wore his new one – and tip-toed down to the kitchen where she filled the kettle and set it on the hob to boil. The range was warm and George put a few sticks and coal in the fire to give it a boost. When their drinks were in front of them, Laura looked at her husband expectantly.

"Go on, then, spit it out."

"I don't know where to start, Laura. I know that what I'm feeling isn't right, but I can't help it. I feel so useless to you. Every time I start having a good time, I feel ill. Last night was the final straw. I don't know why you stay with me. What can I give you except a freezing cold house and poverty? Polly and Chris have so much, and I know I shouldn't feel resentful, but I do. There I've said it."

Laura put her hand over his and looked earnestly into his eyes, "Listen, George. I would rather have a freezing cold house and live on the breadline as long as I have you."

George went to speak, but Laura continued, waving away his objections, "No, George, let me finish. Why would you feel resentful of Polly and Chris? I don't – I'm just glad that they are happy together, and don't forget we have something that they don't. A family, George - Polly would swap places with me tomorrow if she could have a daughter like Emma. If you continue to brood like you have been doing, it'll make us all miserable and you'll make yourself ill. Me and Emma love you. It doesn't matter if we have no money, because we have you. Can't you understand that?"

"No, not really, Laura," he looked around the room and drew in a ragged breath. "I can't seem to get past the fact that I've let you down. When we got married and I was healthy, we had the world at our feet once the war was over, but now – look at me – I can't even give you a pair of boots or Emma a decent present for Christmas! I'm on the scrap heap at thirty-two."

"If you don't pull yourself together and stop blaming yourself, you're going to destroy what little we do have, George. I can't put it plainer than that. I love you with all my heart and I know that once this winter's over, you'll get a job somewhere. I just know it. Please try to buck up, for Emma's sake if not mine."

George studied her face and pondered the intensity of her words, but try as he might, he couldn't shake the dogged depression that threatened to take over his world. "I'll really try, Laura, but I feel so useless. Even chopping a few logs for the fire and shovelling some coal nearly did me in. I'm as weak as a kitten and I hate it."

"But you will get better. Please look forward instead of dwelling on things as they are now."

"Like I said, I'll try."

He managed a small smile but his eyes didn't reflect it. "Let's have another cuppa and see if there's any cake left. Then we'll have to get back to bed. It's only 3 o'clock."

The transport arrived from Brigg later that day to pick up Kurt and return him to the camp. He said his goodbyes and promised to write once he had been repatriated.

"Every Christmas I will remember your hospitality," he said as he climbed into the back of the lorry.

The family relaxed again and Emma enjoyed the attention she received from the grown-ups who played her games and read stories to her. It was a quiet time and Polly and Laura managed to have a few moments together in the kitchen where Polly asked about George's strange mood.

"Take no notice of him, Polly. He's just feeling bad about not being able to work yet, but I've told him to buck up and enjoy these few days."

It was an unsatisfactory answer but it would have to suffice. Polly thought back to the days they had spent in their little house on Beck Hill. Laura had married Sean O'Connell after a brief romance, only to suffer months of abuse at his hands. It was only after he had died in a drowning accident that it was revealed that he already had a wife and four children back in Ireland. George had eventually convinced her of his love for her and they had married at the outbreak of the war. Polly felt that Laura deserved to be happy now and felt a little aggrieved that George was causing her more worry.

The following days allowed George the time he needed to relax, when his mind would let him. He did what he could to help around the house and tried his hardest to be congenial for Laura's sake. He thought she deserved a rest from the never-ending drudgery of home, but he would he heartily glad to return there. At least there was no pretence in his own surroundings and now that he felt better he could look for work. Martin and Antoinette had left to catch a train to London in search of Antoinette's mother, and it was only the five of them left together with Mrs Garside.

Preparations and plans were ongoing for the New Year's Eve party and some of George's family were attending too. Such were his mood swings, that he didn't know if he was looking forward to seeing them or not. His parents were calling in once they'd been to the Volunteer Arms (or Topsy's as it was known locally) which was located across the street and one or two of his brothers and sisters would be dropping by if they could. Polly was looking forward to seeing them again as they had lived next door to the family when they were growing up on Beck Hill. There hadn't been time to catch up with many people since they had returned from Canada so the party was a good opportunity to do just that. Invitations had been sent to some of Polly's school friends too and one or two had responded positively, including Mary Simpson.

The weather was mild for the time of year so once the shops were open again the task of replenishing the larder fell to Polly and Laura. Emma was happy to play in the large garden at the back while they went off for an hour or so, with promises from the men that they would look after her.

"I want to pop in at home, Polly, if you don't mind. We'll be going home soon so I want to make sure that everything is alright. I might event light a fire in the front room to make sure that the chill is taken off the air. The last thing I need is George getting poorly again."

"He's seemed a bit quiet since Christmas, is he alright?"

"I think he feels it because he can't provide for us like he used to."

"Well, it must be a big strain on you all. Is there anything we can do?"

"No, not really. He's not too good at taking charity, as he calls it."

Polly was shocked. "Charity! We wouldn't be offering charity! Does he really think we look down on him and see him as a charity case?"

"He's a very proud man, Polly. He wouldn't even accept help from his own family, let alone you, so don't get upset by him. Just leave things alone."

The rest of the journey down Fleetgate was silent and the walk to Waterside became uneasy. Eventually, Laura spoke up, "Look, Polly. Try to see things from George's point of view. He sees what Chris can give you and the way you live and he thinks he falls short in providing for his own family."

"I suppose so. But we've always been close, Laura, and if I felt we were drifting apart I couldn't bear it."

"We won't drift apart, silly. George will get a job after Christmas and as soon as the new Council houses are built on Freddy Hopper's field then he'll feel a lot better about things."

Polly was mollified by her sister's words but as they entered the kitchen on Humber Terrace the cold, starkness of the little house engulfed them.

"Brrr. Let's get that fire going. It's a good job it's mild outside, at least the pipes won't burst. I hope not anyway".

Half an hour later they were sat in front of the fire with a cup of tea. The Baxter household had provided some milk for them and Dot had promised to light another fire on the morning of the second of January to keep the damp at bay. It would also give them a warm house to come back to.

"Dot Baxter's a bit of a tyrant, but if she's on your side then you couldn't wish for a better friend. She's a nosey old cat at times, but has a heart of gold. There's a few round here who I wouldn't trust with a key, but Dot's not like that."

Polly nodded. She remembered the old days when her parents had died within a couple of years of each other. If it hadn't been for George's mother and father supporting them as they had, they wouldn't have made it through those days. Of course, Sean O'Connell had been there, but he was next to useless at anything except causing trouble.

"Come on. Let's wash these cups and go and see what Mr Lacey has in today. I hope he's got some sugar and flour and we can do a bit of baking to help Mrs Garside out." Laura jumped up from the sofa and went through to the kitchen where she proceeded to put the last of the water out of the kettle into a bowl and wash up their cups.

Polly and Laura entered the little shop just as the last customer was leaving. Lacey's shop, like many others, had an old Victorian frontage and was located at the bottom of Fleetgate opposite the White Swan. Polly was immediately transported back to her youth as she looked around and inhaled the aromas. The shelves at the back of the shop held tinned goods and packets while lower shelves held bleach and disinfectant together with packets of Oxydol and Sunlight soap. Inside it looked as if time had stood still. The long polished wooden counter curved around the full width of the shop, broken only by a flap which allowed access to the front entrance. At one side of the counter, where it curved were two round-backed chairs where customers could sit and chat to each other while they waited for their orders to be made up. Mr Lacey was usually serving while his wife helped out occasionally but her usual job was in the back storage area where chests of tea and bags of flour and sugar were stored. She would make sure the shelves were re-stocked and that the orders were made up properly. The air was heavy with mixed spice and warm bread which was delivered daily from Mr Simpson's bakery on King Street. Hams hung in cloth from beams adding to the ambience.

"Hello, Laura. How are you and the family? Did you have a nice Christmas?" Mrs Lacey came bustling to the front of the shop wearing a white calf length apron with wide straps to the shoulders. "And is this Polly? How are you, love? We haven't seen you for years."

"Hello, Mrs Lacey. We're all well, thanks and home for good, now that the war's over."

Mr Lacey approached the front of the counter and took the list that Laura handed to him. He was a small man with bottle bottom glasses perched on his nose. The magnification made his eyes look huge and Polly was reminded of the times she and Laura had giggled at him when they were children.

"Do you want Kenny to deliver these, Polly?" Mr Lacey asked as he read down the list.

"That would be a great help, please," she replied gratefully.

Five minutes later they were heading up to the High Street where the higgledy-piggledy mix of residential homes and commercial shops leaned against each other in mutual support. The donkey-stoned steps of the houses protruded onto the pavement and Polly remembered neighbours sitting outside and chatting in the summer sun. She longed for some summer sunshine and a return to familiar sights. The war might not have touched Barton much on the outside but many of the people inside the little houses had lost someone they loved, or sheltered the wounded, who would be left to get on with life as best they could.

FIVE

Emma had decided to explore the garden while her mother was out shopping and ventured past the old greenhouse and into the orchard. She played at jumping off a log for a while but soon became bored. She was about to go back to the house when she heard the pitiful mewling of a kitten. Searching around the hedges she could find nothing, but the further she went to the end of the garden the louder the cries became. A wrought iron gate at the end of the orchard separated it from another part of the garden. This looked as if it hadn't been touched for many years and the path which had once meandered through formal flower beds was now very overgrown.

Emma could hear the plaintive cries of the kitten and was determined to find it. Cautiously, and looking back over her shoulder to make sure her father wasn't coming after her, she lifted the catch on the gate and entered this new and exciting world of overgrown shrubbery and mysterious pathways. About halfway down and to the left was a dip in the landscape and following the kitten's urgent mewls she came upon a slime covered pond with sloping earth banks. Balanced precariously on a piece of wood and floating just out of reach was the kitten, a pathetic sight to anyone, but to a little girl of Emma's age - was irresistible. It was a tiny black bundle of wet fur, with two white front feet and a blaze of white on its chest.

She looked around for some way of bringing the creature to dry land and found a stick in the bushes. For a few minutes she leaned over the pool, thick with the slime of years of neglect, reaching as far as she could to try and hook the piece of wood and drag it with its cargo to the edge of the pond. Her efforts were futile so she decided to move further down the bank. The sides were slippery and she hung onto the long grass as she descended but the grass gave no purchase and she fell on her bottom and then slid speedily into the water feet first. Her first thought was that her mother would be angry because she had her new wellingtons on and she could feel them filling with water and mud. Then she remembered she had her school coat on and they couldn't possibly afford to get her another one. The cold water and thick mud sucked her deeper and deeper. She cried out for her father but knew he was in the house, far away from the pond. Twisting one way and then the other trying to escape the clutches of the sucking mud she found herself heavy with water. The kitten brought her attention back to its own predicament and even though she knew her danger, she lifted the cat off the wooden plank it had been clinging to and brought it to the edge of the bank. Her coat was sodden and she began to cry as her boots were sucked off her feet. She could feel the mud drawing her down and screamed for her father. Her heart raced as she imagined never seeing her mother again but then her feet suddenly stopped sinking and she stayed half in and half out of the water. It was very cold but after a while she didn't feel the cold anymore, just tired. The kitten stayed close by and she brought it even closer to gain some comfort from its proximity. Half an hour later she was still there, her clothes were soaked and she thought that maybe if she just closed her eyes for a few minutes and rested, then she would wake up and have the energy to crawl free.

It seemed that she had just closed her eyes when she heard her father shouting to her uncle Chris.

"She's here, Chris. She's fallen in the water."

Emma felt herself lifted gently from her cold, watery prison but she must have gone to sleep again because the next thing she knew she was in a bath of warm water and her mother was washing her clean. She could hear her mother's soothing voice and at once felt at peace. The warm water felt lovely and she drifted off to sleep again.

***

Originally, The Elms, so Chris had told Polly, had been a Georgian mansion but the Victorians had added the top storey as servant's quarters. The house itself stood diagonally opposite Baysgarth Park and fronted onto Whitecross Street. It was an imposing building set on high ground and surrounded by lawns to three sides. High brick walls kept the back of the house private from Barrow Road on one side and Caistor Road on the other. Polly smiled to herself as she remembered her humble beginnings as a nursery maid with the Beauchamp family.

She and Laura were totally unprepared for what met them as they entered the kitchen through the back door. Mrs Garside was weeping inconsolably, throwing her apron over her head one minute and pulling it back the next. Laura stood frozen at the door as she watched George, holding what appeared to be the lifeless body of her daughter.

"What's going on? What's happened?" Polly asked as she stood pale-faced, the shopping bags discarded on the kitchen floor.

"Emma!" The strangled, tortured voice emanating from Laura was alien to those who heard it.

Emma's eyes flickered for a moment in recognition of her name and Laura ran to her side. The little girl's dress was covered in pond slime, and weed tangled her hair.

"She fell in the pond, Polly," Chris explained.

"How long has she been like this?" Laura looked at George for an answer.

"We only found her five minutes ago. We were trying to warm her up."

"Give her to me." Laura took charge of her daughter and signalled for Polly to help.

Polly was beside her in a flash. Emma's face was ashen and her eyes closed to the world. The only sign of life was a slight pulse in her neck as it lolled from side to side as she was lifted from her father's knee. Between them she was half carried and half dragged up the stairs and into a bathroom. Polly ran a warm bath while Laura gently undressed her daughter and between them they lay her in the water. After a time the colour began to seep back into Emma's body and Laura held her head, all the time talking to her while she washed her with scented soap. Polly hurried to the airing cupboard and found warm towels to wrap her in and within half an hour she was tucked up in bed with her mother waiting anxiously for a sign of recovery.

Polly returned to the kitchen on shaking legs now that they had done all they could. Mrs Garside had recovered herself a little and was busy making a hot drink and Chris was putting the shopping away. George hadn't moved.

"You'd better go up to Laura, George. Take her a cup of tea." Polly touched him lightly on the shoulder but it took him a few seconds to respond. He looked blankly up at her from his chair.

"Upstairs, George. Go up to Laura and Emma."

"Oh, right." He took the proffered cup from Mrs Garside and left the kitchen by the back stairs, his trembling legs hardly managing to carry him up.

"What happened?" Polly looked at Chris for an explanation.

"We were playing darts in the dining room and Emma was playing in the garden. We didn't see much harm could come to her out there, and never thought she'd let herself through the gate. I didn't think she would go all the way down there. When she didn't answer our calls to come in for a drink, George went to find her. She had slid down the side of the bank and was laid half in, and half out of the water. I don't know how long she had been there. It would appear that she was trying to rescue that." He pointed to the tiny black and white kitten now tucked up in a cardboard box by the side of the range, its tiny tongue trying to remove the mud drying quickly on its fur. "She was clutching it to her when we found her."

Chris dragged his hair back with both hands and paced up and down the kitchen. "I'll never forgive myself if anything happens to that little girl, Polly. Never!"

"I think we should ring the doctor, don't you?" she answered.

"Yes, of course. I'll go and do it now."

Dr Birtwhistle lived about five minutes away on Priestgate, so arrived at The Elms in no time. Laura and George stood at the foot of Emma's bed and watched as the doctor listened to her chest with his stethoscope. Her face was flushed and beads of perspiration were beginning to form on her forehead. Her breathing was shallow and the only sign of life was the occasional twitching of her eyelids as she lay prone between the white cotton sheets.

"Will she be alright, doctor?" George's voice was hushed as if almost reluctant to hear the answer.

"It's hard to tell at the moment, Mr Taylor. I'll leave her something to help bring her temperature down and call back tomorrow morning."

"Can she be moved? George asked, deliberately not looking at Laura. She snapped her head round quickly in surprise, but the doctor had started to reply before she collected her thoughts.

"I'll let you know tomorrow." He delved into the depths of his black medical bag and brought out a bottle of red liquid which he handed to Laura.

"Three teaspoons of this every four hours and through the night. Can you manage that, Mrs Taylor?"

"Yes, of course."

"I'll call in tomorrow morning. Keep her warm but not overheated. You can open a window during the day but close it at night."

He looked into the eyes of the worried parents and took a deep breath. "Try not to worry. We'll just have to wait and see what the morning brings."

Polly and Chris were waiting at the bottom of the stairs as he came down into the hallway. She repeated the questions her sister and brother-in-law had asked and received the same reply. As he picked up his hat to leave, Chris said, "Please send me your bill, doctor. If we need a nurse I'll make sure Emma has one."

His words were almost cut off in mid-stream. George was halfway down the stairs as he roared, "Oh, no you don't. If there's any bills to pay I'll pay them, and if *my* daughter needs a nurse then her mother will do the nursing. I'm sick to death of having your money shoved down my throat."

The doctor closed the door quietly as he left, leaving Chris in shock and Polly in tears. "Look, George – I didn't mean…."

"You never *do* mean, do you Chris? You're so damned clever at hand outs and such. Well, this time you can keep it. As soon as we hear what Emma's condition is tomorrow we're leaving."

Polly reached out to George as she approached him, trying to calm him down. "Please, George. I'm begging you to think about this. Wait a few days until Emma is getting better before thinking about leaving. Please." Her voice broke as the final word left her mouth and she dissolved into Chris's arms. George turned away and went back up the stairs.

Chris took Polly into the living room and sat her down on the sofa. Mrs Garside must have heard the exchange from the kitchen and appeared with a tea tray which Chris indicated with a nod that she should leave on the side table. When she had left the room, Chris poured a strong cup of tea into a china cup and handed it to Polly who took it with shaking fingers.

"I can't believe that just happened, Chris. What have we done wrong?"

"I think he's worried out of his mind, Polly. There's nothing we can do until the doctor has been tomorrow, so I suggest we just carry on as normal and let George and Laura alone to sort themselves out."

Just then the door opened quietly and Mrs Garside came in. Both heads turned in her direction and she hovered uncertainly before speaking, "It's just that I was thinking about the party. Should we cancel it? I mean – nobody's going to be in the mood for celebrating are they?"

"You're quite right, Mrs Garside. Thanks for thinking about that," Chris answered quickly before Polly could intervene. "We need to let everyone know what has happened and quickly."

"If you can let me have the guest list, I can send word to everyone. My neighbour's lad, Stanley, has a bike and can cover ground pretty quickly, especially if there's sixpence in it for him."

Polly went to the writing bureau in the corner of the room and held out a list with names and addresses written neatly one under the other. "Thank you, Mrs Garside. I expect George's relatives will come once they hear so there might be a few cups of tea to make."

"That's never been a problem, Polly. I'll go round now and ask if he can do it as soon as possible."

"I'll ring the ones with telephones," Chris added. "There aren't many but it will make it easier for the lad."

The comings and goings over the next few hours kept Polly and Mrs Garside running to and from the kitchen trying to keep up with requests for supplies of tea. Laura ventured down into the living room to sit withdrawn, trying to answer the constant questions as to why this had happened. George was noticeable by his absence, but no one commented, assuming that he wanted to stay near to his daughter. Mr and Mrs Taylor senior were supportive, and encouraged Laura to look on the bright side, but after they had looked in on Emma and George, they came out again less sure than before. George's sister, Eve and her husband Raymond, popped in for a few minutes, but Eve was expecting their first child and Raymond was solicitous about her overtiring herself and they left after half an hour. Polly looked enviously at Eve's obvious pregnancy and even though her thoughts were with Emma, she couldn't help wishing she was in the same condition. Eventually, though, the straggle of visitors ceased and Polly and Chris were able to retire for the night, although without much hope of sleep. Laura was just trying to get some of the medicine the doctor had left with her into Emma's mouth as Polly put her head round the door for the last time that night.

"How is she?" Polly asked, hoping for a positive response.

"Just the same really, but very restless now. She hasn't woken up yet and her face and forehead are burning up." Laura's voice wobbled with emotion as she answered.

Polly could see George sitting at the other side of the bed. He hadn't acknowledged her at all when she had entered the room.

"If there is anything you need, Laura. Just come and get me."

"Alright, Polly, but I don't think there's anything you can do. Me and George will watch her, so you go to bed."

"Goodnight, Laura. Goodnight, George." There was only Laura's reply.

**

Waiting for the doctor the following morning seemed as endless as the previous sleepless night. Emma was still unconscious but Laura had managed to force some of the medicine down her throat which had helped her to have a restful sleep. Laura and George looked hollowed-eyed and exhausted, but George still refused to leave his daughter's bedside. He drank endless cups of tea but spoke to no one except Laura.

Dr Birtwhistle took the stairs two at a time as fast as his long legs allowed. His examination was thorough and he made notes on a card which he threw into his bag on completion.

"Emma needs to go to hospital," he announced. "She has to be kept under observation for a few days and they have easier access to the necessary drugs. I'll go down and call an ambulance now."

George and Laura looked bewildered as he left the room without further comment.

"Oh, George!" Laura wailed. "She's going into hospital. What are we going to do?"

"We'll go with her of course," he snapped. Their long anxious night was telling on both of them and their nerves were stretched to breaking point.

Laura sobbed into her handkerchief as she approached the top of the stairs. She looked down at the doctor as he spoke softly into the telephone. Chris and Polly were standing at the living room door waiting to find out what was going on. Polly looked up the stairs and caught sight of her sister looking as she had never seen her before. She broke away from Chris and mounted the stairs, reaching out to Laura who walked into her arms and sobbed on Polly's shoulder. Together they descended the stairs and reached the bottom just as the doctor put the telephone receiver down.

"The ambulance will be here soon, Mrs Taylor. I suggest you put a few of Emma's things in a bag while you're waiting."

"Which hospital will she be going to, doctor?" Laura asked brokenly.

"Scunthorpe for now, we'll have to wait and see what the doctors' say when they've examined her. You can travel with her in the ambulance but you will need to get the bus back."

"We'll follow in the car," Chris smiled as he touched Laura's shoulder, "then we can bring you back."

Laura started to smile her acceptance but was halted by George, "That won't be necessary, thank you. We'll manage. Emma's our daughter and we don't need you trailing along."

"Surely you'll let us come, George. Emma's our niece and we love her very much." Polly was astounded at George's stubbornness.

The ambulance men arrived at that moment and Laura and George went with them to show them the way. Two minutes later they came down with their coats on. Emma was being carried on a stretcher, still fast asleep and covered in blankets. Her little flushed face made Polly try one more time.

"Please, George. Please let us come. Think about Laura and all the travelling. You're both exhausted."

George looked at his wife and then back at Polly and nodded reluctantly. "Go on then," was all he said.

SIX

It was ten weeks since Emma's accident and although she was out of hospital she had been removed to a convalescent home for children in Hornsea. The diagnosis was polio and both Polly and Chris were devastated at the news that she had lost the use of her right leg and her left leg was very weak. The Ministry of Health had been called in to test the water in the pond and had found it contaminated with raw sewage. Further investigations had discovered a leaking pipe from an old cess pit had caused the pond water to fester for years. It had been an accident waiting to happen and poor little Emma had been the innocent victim.

When George found out the reason he refused to speak to either Chris or Polly and told Laura she wasn't to see Polly either. Despite pleas from Laura, he wouldn't change his mind and out of loyalty she complied. Polly's worst nightmare had come to pass and she was estranged from her beloved sister. Her inner loneliness continued unabated and the bleak, severity of the winter snows cut her off even further. She had become so depressed that she gave little attention to the fact that her periods had stopped. At first she put it down to the shock of Emma's accident and then had forgotten about it. She suffered emotionally and mentally without Laura's support, even though Chris had taken full responsibility and had the pond drained, the pipe removed and the cess pit emptied and filled in. To George it was all too little, and far too late.

It was Mrs Garside who noticed Polly had thickened around the waistline, despite the fact that she hadn't eaten much since the accident. Since Emma's admittance to hospital Polly had eaten only sparingly as the sight of food made her feel sick, which everyone had put down to her fretting. Now, Mrs Garside was having second thoughts and drew a deep breath before mentioning the fact.

"Are you feeling like eating today, Polly?"

"No, not really. I'll have a slice of toast if we've any bread, but I don't want anything much," she answered despondently.

"I was wondering…"

"Wondering what?" Polly asked when she noticed the sentence had tapered off.

"Well, you've not been eating much but you seem to be putting on weight."

Polly looked down at her stomach which appeared a little rounder than usual. Her blouse too had begun to gape slightly as the buttons stretched across her bust.

"Have you had your monthly visitor lately?"

"Come to think of it, no. I haven't been taking much notice. I've been so worried about Emma."

"I think a visit to the doctor is in order, don't you?" Mrs Garside smiled as the implications of their conversation sank in.

Polly smiled for the first time in months. The old sparkle came into her eyes momentarily before dying once again as she thought of having a baby at this time. She was torn between euphoria and guilt but couldn't wait for Chris to come home at lunchtime so that she could tell him of their suspicions.

Chris had decided on a teaching career and with his qualifications gained from private schooling before the war, he found no difficulty in finding work at the Church School where both Polly and Laura and lately, Emma had attended. He had been there two weeks and loved every minute. The other teachers were amiable and the headmaster strict but fair. He had taken to coming home at lunchtime to check on Polly, knowing how she missed her sister's company. If the weather was too bad he stayed in school but he had been known to battle through a blizzard to get back to her. The snow was thigh deep in places and some of the younger children stayed away, but the older ones had great fun having snowball fights in the playground. Occasionally, he had to take his turn doing playground duty and fell victim to a few snowballs when his back was turned. He would have loved to have joined in but felt it unwise to encourage the boys – not that they needed any encouragement.

On this particular day he arrived back at The Elms around lunch time to find Polly pacing up and down the living room in front of the fire. He just managed to get his coat off before she threw herself into his arms.

"Oh, Chris, guess what? I think I'm expecting... or at least Mrs Garside does."

"Really! That's wonderful news, Polly. Have you been to see the doctor?"

"I've telephoned him and I'm going later on today. I'm so excited I can't sit still."

"It's about time we had some good news." Chris laughed and picked Polly up and spun her round and round until she begged him to stop. They were both breathless as he fell onto the sofa with her and pulled her onto his lap, kissing her neck and hugging her tightly.

Polly didn't know whether to laugh or cry but her laughter suddenly turned to tears and she sobbed into her husband's shoulder.

"Hey, why the tears? Aren't you happy?"

"Course I am," she sniffed, "it's just that I feel so guilty for being happy when Emma is still poorly, and I want to talk to Laura about it all but I can't."

Chris rubbed her back lovingly and allowed her to have a good cry. Eventually, the torrent ended and she looked at him with weepy eyes.

"I'm sorry. It's just been so unexpected. I didn't even know myself until Mrs Garside said I was putting weight on."

"I haven't noticed either, so it's as big a surprise to me as it is to you."

Polly pushed his hair back as it flopped forward and looked lovingly into his eyes. "Won't it be lovely, Chris - a baby of our very own."

"More than lovely," he replied huskily. "What shall we call it?"

"I don't know. I haven't given that a thought. We'll talk about it tonight, shall we?"

Chris looked at the clock and realised he had very little time in which to eat his lunch. "Come on. Let's go down to the kitchen and see what Mrs Garside has for me today then I'll have to get back to school."

Back at school, the afternoon dragged as his mind was with Polly and how she was faring at the doctors. Could it be true that they were going to be parents after all this time? His thoughts roamed to Waterside and Humber Terrace where he imagined Laura and George would be anxiously awaiting news of their own daughter. He felt so guilty about the pond and the accident but didn't know how to make amends. It was only when an ink blot was fired from someone's ruler and it hit the blackboard behind him that he realised he hadn't been concentrating on his class. Stifled giggles were emanating from behind small hands clutching at mouths as Chris jumped out of his skin. It wouldn't do to be found daydreaming by the headmaster after only two weeks. He decided to concentrate on matters in hand but ignored the ink blot which slowly slid down the blackboard and plopped onto the floor bringing forth more sniggers from the boys. Just then the bell rang for playtime and he dismissed the class for ten minutes while they went outside to play in the snow.

He decided not to go and join the other teachers in the staff room for a cup of tea, but instead cleaned up the blot of paper and threw it into the waste paper bin. The next thing he did was plan his revenge on the children – he couldn't let them get away with disrupting the classroom, although he really wanted to join in and laugh with them. Instead, he set them a blackboard full of sums, at which they all groaned when they filed back into the classroom.

"We were going to do something else for the last hour or so before you go home," he informed the pupils, "but to repay you for the ink blot," he glared at the boys under furrowed brows, "you can do these sums and put your hands up when you've finished."

There was a general groan from around the room and Chris turned back to the blackboard with a grin on his face. A rustle of paper followed and a few accusatory whispers in the direction of the culprit, but by the time Chris turned around again, all heads were bent over their task, a few of them chewing the ends of their pencils. The ink blot incident didn't recur in Mr Beauchamp's class again.

Chris wandered up and down the aisles between the desks which looked as if they had seen better days, and thought back to his first day when he heard of the school's designer, Samuel Wilderspin. He had been a great educational reformer of the Victorian age, introducing new teaching methods which were designed to reach every child. Originally, gas lamps had hung from the ceilings but these had been replaced by electricity and the original steps in the infant's classroom had been removed and desks installed, but the fireplace was still being used. There had been a few improvements since it had been built in 1844, like the toilet block in the playground, but the fabric of the school itself was unchanged.

One by one the children put their pencils down and put their hands up. Chris sat down behind his desk and beckoned them, one by one, to bring their work up to the front where he marked them in red ink. He made a note of the marks in his book and this way he could see at a glance which pupils needed more help than others.

At last the head boy could be heard ringing the hand bell which was kept outside the headmaster's study and everyone, including Chris, breathed a sigh of relief. He couldn't wait to get back to Polly to find out what the doctor had said.

He stepped outside into a bitterly cold north wind which was blowing snow into drifts against the houses. March was always a windy month, but this one bit to the bone as he put his head down and leaned forward in order to make some headway. He felt sorry for the poorer children who had only hand-me-down jackets to wear if they were lucky. Others made do with a couple of jumpers, one over the other, and ran as fast they could to get home.

Chris stepped into the hallway and stamped his feet on the coconut matting before bending to remove his shoes. He was almost frozen stiff after the cold walk home, but was longing to hear Polly's news. He didn't have long to wait as she burst out of the living room and threw herself into his arms, laughing as she did so. "You're going to be a dad, Chris. We're going to have a baby!" She leaned back to see his reaction and wasn't disappointed. The look on his face told her all she needed to know. He was ecstatic at the news and held her to him in a gentle embrace. They stayed that way for a long moment before he finished taking off his coat and led her into the living room where he stood before the fire to try and get some feeling back into his legs.

"You are pleased, aren't you, Chris?" Polly asked nervously. He still hadn't spoken.

"Of course I am, silly. It's just such a surprise isn't it? I mean, this morning when I went to work it was just another day, and now, we're going to have another little person in the house. I'm just a bit overwhelmed, that's all." He went to sit beside her on the sofa and took her hands in his own. He turned her wedding ring around with his thumb and watched the gold sparkle in the firelight. "I love you more than I can say, Polly. This is just the icing on the cake, isn't it?"

Tears sprang to Polly's eyes as she looked into her husband's kind, and generous face. She knew he had always loved her, but tonight his gaze held so much promise for the future, and although she had always loved him, she began to understand the meaning of marriage. "I love you so much too, Chris. I don't know what I'd do without you."

He smiled and kissed her lips. "Let's hope you never have to find out then." He moved away for a second before grinning, "now then – what's for tea. I'm starving!"

SEVEN

At the same time as Polly and Chris were celebrating their news, Laura was still trying to come to terms with the fact that her precious little girl had polio. It was a mild case, but nevertheless, traumatic for all concerned. Her right leg was encased in a calliper and her left leg was thinner and weaker than before. Visiting her in Scunthorpe hospital had been bad enough but if Emma's condition had worsened she would have had to have gone to Sheffield. As it was she had spent some time in the convalescent home in Hornsea where she had undergone an exercise routine. The doctors were hopeful that she may be able to walk again if she continued to improve.

Laura sat at the end of Emma's bed and watched her once robust daughter sleeping. She thought back to the time the doctors had given their diagnosis and it had seemed like a death knell. George had taken it very badly and had blamed everyone – Chris and Polly for not draining the pond, Laura for going shopping, but mostly he blamed himself. Laura remembered the countless conversations when he almost drove her mad with incessant accusations and 'what ifs'.

The weather had been atrocious. The news on the wireless said it was the worst winter in living memory. Snow had fallen, constantly it seemed, since the middle of January which had made visiting Emma difficult at best, and at times impossible. Laura had given up her part-time job at Hoppers but fortunately, and to George's relief, as well as her own, he had found work in Hull as a welder. This meant he had to leave home very early in the morning to catch the train to New Holland where the ferry would be waiting to transport workers over the Humber. In the sub-zero temperatures, even the river had frozen at times and more than once he had been forced to take shelter in Hull rather than make the journey home. This job had restored his self-confidence to a large degree but his mental state was tenuous and his physical condition although improved, was not good, but he was determined to hold this job down for his family's sake. Emma's illness had drained him emotionally which gave him the ideal opportunity to distance himself from Chris, who although he knew in the depths of his being, was completely innocent of all charges, George used as his whipping boy.

Laura stood at the bedroom window and looked out over the Waterside area. It was on low-lying land and prone to flooding, so she was dreading the time when all the snow would begin to melt and couldn't wait to move into a new council house near to where George's parents lived on Ramsden Avenue. Freddie Hopper had sold the field to the council and quite a few houses were planned. She hoped that later in the year would find them once more on the move, but this time in happier circumstances.

She was brought out of her reverie by movement from the bed behind her. Emma was waking up and Laura never ceased to be amazed at the stoicism of her young daughter. She hated the calliper, and who could blame her, but she constantly looked forward to the day when she would be well enough and strong enough not to need it.

"Hello, sleepy head," Laura smiled.

"Hello, mam. Is dad back yet?"

"He won't be long. Do you want to get up and have some tea with us? You could put your feet up on the settee in the living room."

"Oooh, yes please."

Laura drew back the bedding and helped Emma to stand somewhat unsteadily before lifting her gently and taking her downstairs to the living room where a fire burned brightly, dispelling the air of gloom which penetrated from the outside. Night had fallen quickly and the sky looked heavy with snow again.

"Mam," Emma began. "When are Aunty Polly and Uncle Chris coming to see us? We haven't seen them for ages, have we?"

Laura swallowed uncomfortably and looked into Emma's trusting eyes. "Maybe you'd better ask your dad," was the only answer she could give her without giving free rein to the resentment she felt towards her husband.

"What about the little kitten, mam. Can I keep him?"

"I think Aunty Polly is keeping it for you, love."

"Well, when the weather's better maybe we can go and see him." Again, Emma managed, without contrivance, to twist Laura's emotions into knots as she thought about Polly. How she missed her little sister. Inwardly, she blamed George for their estrangement while outwardly she tried to be a loyal wife by acceding to her husband's wishes, but she burned with resentment and every instinct told her that his intransigence made no sense whatsoever.

"Yes, love. Maybe in the spring when the weather is nicer, we'll go and see him."

Just then the back door opened and George walked in, looking paler than he had been for weeks. Laura went through to the kitchen and helped him off with his coat, taking his canvas bag which held his thermos flask and sandwich box which he took to work every day. "Have you had a good day?" Laura asked stiffly.

"Not too bad," was the stock answer as he brushed past her but his eyes lit up at seeing Emma on the sofa.

"How's my little angel today?" he asked. Laura noticed how his expression changed and the colour came back to his face as he kissed his daughter's cheek.

"I'm alright, ta, dad. I was wondering why Aunty Polly and Uncle Chris haven't been to see us. Mam said that we might be able to go and see the kitten when the weather's better. Can we, dad?"

The question was so guileless and took him so completely by surprise that George looked at Laura as if he had been hit with a cricket bat. Laura on the other hand walked back into the kitchen to get on with preparing their meal and left him to it. She was secretly quite pleased he had been put on the spot, and wondered how he was going to explain his actions to his daughter.

The potatoes were boiling in the saucepan when George returned to the kitchen looking sheepish. Laura was expecting some kind of comment but George was subdued and he sighed heavily before climbing the stairs to get changed out of his working clothes. She didn't know whether this was a good sign or not but then she heard a whimper from the living room and flew to the source. She found Emma hugging a cushion trying to stifle her sobs. Laura sat beside her and held her little body tightly, trying to comfort the little girl and at the same time hold onto her temper.

George was being so stubborn and she couldn't believe he had upset his daughter into the bargain.

Between sniffles, Emma said, "Dad says it was Aunty Polly's and Uncle Chris's fault that I fell in the water and got poorly, mam. But it wasn't – I wanted to save the kitten and it was my fault, not theirs. Now he won't let me see them." On this note she began to wail again.

"Never mind, love, hush up and I'll try and talk to your dad again tonight. Come on, stop crying or you won't want your tea."

Gradually, Emma stopped crying and Laura went back into the kitchen, seething inside that her husband could be so stupidly stubborn. She most certainly would have words with him later that evening once Emma was back in bed.

George came down the stairs and Laura couldn't look at him so she missed the hurt expression in his eyes as he approached her. He tried to pull her into his embrace, but for once she stood firm and kept her back towards him.

"Do you want a hand putting the tea out?" he asked, trying to make amends.

"No thank you."

"Shall I put the kettle on then?"

"No."

"Look, Laura....."

"Not now, George. Emma will hear."

"I'm going down the yard then."

Laura didn't reply and continued to busy herself in the kitchen as he stepped outside the back door. The wind was still blowing a gale as he walked gingerly on the compacted ice which the local children had made into lethal slides. He sat in the toilet block for some time smoking a cigarette, until he heard someone else in the next cubicle coughing and spluttering. The sound of a newspaper being opened told him that the occupant was probably intending to be there for some time, but he still didn't move. Luckily he had thought to put his coat on before he left the house and he hugged it to himself for extra warmth, as his breath condensed in the cold air. Thoughts were teeming around his brain as he sat staring at the old, pock-marked, wooden door in front of him. The look on Emma's face when he had told her that Polly and Chris weren't welcome at their house would break his heart forever. In the short time they had been home, Emma had formed a close attachment to her aunt and uncle, and George was forced to confront his fears that he was jealous. Perhaps Laura was right and he should let it go, but the thought of Emma's illness still riled him when he thought of how that pond had lain stagnant for years. His stubborn streak returned to swamp his senses, and he convinced himself that he was right and they must keep both Chris and Polly at a distance.

**

Later that evening after Emma was in bed, George put the wireless on and listened to the news while Laura washed the dishes. They had hardly spoken to each other since his return from the toilet block and Emma had picked up on their silence, but said nothing. She was an intelligent girl and her illness hadn't affected her senses as far as trouble was concerned. She had asked to go back to bed quite early, feeling guilty that she had caused the unease by asking questions. She loved her mam and dad but couldn't understand why her dad was refusing to listen to her when she told him it had been her own fault she had fallen into the water.

Laura, on the other hand, was determined to get to the bottom of George's problem and as soon as she was sure Emma had dropped off to sleep she started and George was expecting it.

"What on earth has got into you, George? How could you upset Emma so soon after she's come home? Just what has got into you?"

"You know what's got into me, Laura. It's that sister of yours and her lah-di-dah husband, that's what. That pond should have been drained years ago, but no, it was left there for Emma to fall into and now look what's happened – she's an invalid."

"Rubbish. You're talking clap-trap and you know it. To start with it's not even their house, it belongs to Chris's dad, and the military had it for years during the war. So, how could either of them know what was going on at the bottom of the garden? Emma herself admits that she shouldn't have gone through the gate at the bottom, but she did and it's no-one's fault. It was an accident, George, and the sooner you accept that the better for all of us."

"It should have been sorted out years ago. I can't believe you're sticking up for them, Laura. Where's your loyalty?"

"I'll be loyal, George, *when* and *if* it's deserved. We've been through a lot as a family, and we've got through it together, but this time I can't stick up for you because I think you're wrong. For goodness sake, George, they've been out of the country for six years. How were they supposed to know the pond was unsafe?"

"I'm not discussing it any more, Laura. I've made myself quite clear. I'm off out for a drink at the Sloop. I might get some peace there."

Laura was amazed as he stood up and donned his coat yet again. George wasn't much of a drinker and never went out in the week, but she couldn't bring herself to object. Nothing else was said between them and she thought that if Emma hadn't been in bed, he would have slammed the back door as he went out. This was so out of character she found herself starting to worry about him again.

George was fuming when he entered the smoky interior of the Sloop Inn. A lot of the regular Watersiders had already settled at the tables for a night of dominoes and cards. George nodded to a few people he knew but wasn't in the mood for company, so he stayed at the corner of the bar by the wall, hoping he wouldn't be noticed while he sank his first pint of bitter quickly, and then nursed another one, sipping it regularly, but knowing he had little money, he made it last.

"Hey, George, mate." George looked around to find Pud Ouldridge calling to him from one of the tables. "Come on over. Doggy's just gone out the back but he'll be back in a mo. Fancy a game of cards?"

George pushed himself off the bar and reluctantly took his pint over to the table. "Not really in the mood, Pud."

"What's up? Had a barney with that wife of yours?"

"You might say so. Why do women have to be such hard work?"

"I know. Can't live with 'em, can't kill 'em. In't that what the Yanks used to say?"

"Aye, something like that." George found himself smiling in spite of himself.

"What's she done then? – Oh, here comes Doggy."

George nodded to his old friend Doggy Barker as he returned to the table. It seemed everyone in Barton had nicknames that stuck with you as you got older. George and all his siblings had been known as 'Tallywag Taylor' during their childhood, but this had later been shortened to 'Tag' though it wasn't used so much now.

"Now then, George. How's the job going?"

"Good, thanks, and thanks again for putting a word in for me with the gaffer."

"That's alright, mate. You were a good welder before the war, so I didn't see any reason why you couldn't be again."

"Well, let me buy you both a drink anyway. To say thanks, like."

"Thanks, George – I'll have a bottle of brown ale and Doggy here likes a pint of mild."

"I'll just have half a pint though, George. It's cold out there and I don't want to be trotting off out the back too often."

George smiled and returned to the bar to order the drinks. He had just enough money to pay for the drinks and thanked the good Lord that it was pay day on Thursdays.

When he got back to the table, Doggy began, "Pud here tells me you've had a row with the missus, is that right George?"

George raised an eyebrow at Pud before answering, "Just a few words that's all."

"What about?"

"You're like an old gossip sat there, Doggy. What do you want to know for?"

"Thought we might be able to help, that's all George. What are mates for, eh?"

George relented and told them about the trouble with Chris and Polly and how Emma's accident happened. Once he got going he couldn't stop and he found himself getting more and more indignant as he sank his third pint. After his tirade against Chris had ended he leaned back in his seat and waited for a response.

"Well.... wouldn't you be mad if your daughter had caught polio from somebody else's filth?" he said when no comment was forthcoming from either of them.

"Er... well I suppose so, yes." This came from Pud who tried to side with his friend, while Doggy mulled over his answer before replying.

"Wasn't your sister and brother-in-law out of the country for years, George?"

"What's that got to do with it," he snapped.

Doggy looked a little confused, "Well, if they didn't know the water was bad, how could they do something about it?"

Pud tried to signal over George's head that they were on dodgy ground here, but Doggy continued.

"Look at it like this, George. That house that you live in used to belong to the coastguard, didn't it?"

"Yes, all of them did, but what's that got to do with anything?"

"Well, if one of the men who worked for the coastguard years ago, had put up a new door and it fell off while you were living in the house, would it be his fault or would it be yours?"

"It wouldn't be anyone's fault. It would be one of those things that happen."

"That's my point, George. These things happen and it's nobody's fault."

Doggy's analogy was a bit baffling in its simplicity but gradually George let it sink in. His mind shied away from accepting the fact but gradually, he understood what Laura and Emma had been saying. The accident had been no-one's fault. In fact, if anyone was to blame it was him for not keeping an eye on Emma in the first place.

He ran his hands through his black curls and sat back in the hard wooden seat, exhaling and smiling at the same time.

"Anybody getting another round in?" he asked without further comment.

EIGHT

Polly was amazed when she opened the front door the next day to a young lad of about nine years old whom she recognised vaguely as someone she had seen down Waterside. She thought she had seen him from around the Humber Terrace area and her suspicions were confirmed when he looked up to reveal a runny nose and watery eyes which he wiped on the sleeve of his jacket. His fair hair poked out from beneath a grey home-knitted helmet which covered his head, ears and most of his face. He handed her a note.

"Thanks. Is it Eddie?" she asked as she took the note from his extended fingers. He was Dot Baxter's youngest son.

"Yeah. Mrs Taylor asked me to bring you this. She said you might give me tuppence for bringing it."

The young boy looked hopefully at Polly as she turned the letter over in her hand. It was Laura's writing on the envelope, so she tore it open there and then, eagerly scanning the page for words of reconciliation. What she read brought a lump to her throat and looking at the cold little boy in front of her she decided to ask him inside.

"Come on in, Eddie. Do you want a cup of cocoa before you go back home?"

"Cor, yes please, missus. Can I bring my bike in?"

"Not in the front door. Take it round the back and I'll come down and meet you there."

Eddie grinned and Polly noticed his nose had two long green candlesticks emerging again before he sniffed them back up, and she smiled at him, remembering her own impoverished childhood.

After giving Mrs Garside instructions to provide the lad with a cup of cocoa and a piece of cake, she left him happily in front of the glowing range in the kitchen, handing him two pennies as a reward for bringing the long awaited and very welcome note, together with a handkerchief which she told him to keep. She had no doubt that Laura had given him a penny or two before sending him, but she was so delighted to get the letter she didn't care. George had apparently relented unexpectedly and Laura was free to see her sister at any time during the week, but weekends were out of bounds as George would be home. He might have relented in one respect but he still didn't want to have any personal contact with them. Better still, Emma was home. Polly was disappointed that George was still holding a grudge, but hastily wrote a note back to Laura which Eddie could take back with him.

"Dear Laura
I have your note and I can't tell you how happy I am that we can see each other again. I'll come round on Monday and I have some news for you too.
Love Polly xxx"

She hastily stuffed the letter into an envelope and just managed to catch Eddie before he left. He promised to deliver the letter straight away and he picked up his old, rusty bike and rode away.

"Isn't it great news, Mrs Garside. Laura said I can go round on Monday and see Emma. She's home from the convalescent home. I can't wait to see her. I'm going to find Chris and tell him."

She didn't wait to hear what Mrs Garside had to say, but took the kitchen steps two at a time in her eagerness to tell Chris her news. She found him in his study next to the formal dining room surrounded by school books. As it was a Saturday he was catching up on some marking and looked up as Polly dashed in.

"What's the matter, Polly.   Have we won the pools?"

"Don't be daft. I've had a letter – look". She handed over the note and he read it with a sigh of relief.

"Well, isn't that good news? When are you going to see her?"

"Monday, I can't wait any longer. It seems longer than three months since we've seen them."

"Remember your own condition, Polly. I want you to take the car – you learned how to drive in Canada so it shouldn't be a problem for you. I don't want you to have to walk all that way, especially in this weather."

"Don't worry. The weather's getting better every day. I could do with the exercise. I feel as if I've been cooped up indoors for ages. It's alright for you, you get to go out to work."

"I know, but be careful, that's all I'm saying. According to the papers you've got a year to get your provisional licence converted to a full one, otherwise you'll have to take a test."

Polly knew that Chris had her best interests at heart but the last three months had kept her imprisoned, albeit in luxury compared to others, and she wanted to have a look at the shops on the way to Waterside. During the bad weather Chris had insisted that she or Mrs Garside telephoned the grocery order into the shop, which had on occasions been a blessing. Now she wanted to breathe some fresh air and felt restless as the days began lengthening and beckoned her out into the frosty sunshine.

***

It was only on the Monday morning when she set foot outside the house that Polly realised how difficult it was going to be to walk all the way down to Humber Terrace, but nevertheless, she negotiated the steps at the side of the house and made her way to the High Street via the Market Place. She had taken care to dress smartly wearing a pillar box red, tunic-style jacket with a matching skirt. A beret in the same colour sat at a jaunty angle, a pin in the shape of a butterfly held it in place atop her shiny dark hair. The sun was up and the stiff wind brought colour to her cheeks. The snow had turned to slush and was compacted in places but showed signs of melting as she walked. By the time she reached Waterside she was breathing heavily and had a stitch in her left side, so she was very relieved to see the L-shaped row of houses come into view. She knocked on the back door of Laura's house and gingerly pushed it open when her knock remained unanswered.

"Laura?" she called hesitantly.

"I'm upstairs, Polly. Come on up."

Polly climbed the stairs and found Laura trying to help Emma out of bed. Polly gulped back tears when she saw how thin the little girl's legs had become and tried not to look at the calliper which Laura was reaching for. Emma's eyes lit up with pleasure when she saw her aunt.

"Hello, Aunty Polly. You look lovely, doesn't she, mam?" her wide smile showing the gap where her front milk teeth had fallen out recently. Laura nodded her agreement and leaned over to kiss Polly on the cheek. Polly looked happily at the two of them and moved over to the bed to kiss and hug Emma.

"Hello, my darling. How are you?"

"I'm alright, thank you. Mam says I can get up and sit with you while you have a cup of tea. She's made some buns as well."

"Aren't we lucky then?"

Laura stood up and helped Emma to her feet while Polly looked on helplessly, then as Laura was about to lift her daughter, Polly stepped forward and took one of Emma's arms.

"Shall I take one arm and you the other? We can maybe manage easier between us."

Emma was able to move one foot in front of the other in a dragging motion, with the support on both sides and very slowly they got her to the top of the stairs.

"Mam, it hurts my arms like this. Can I shuffle down the stairs on my bottom?"

"If you think you can manage it, but I'll go first shall I?" Laura answered uncertainly.

It was painful to watch Emma trying to slide down the stairs in this way but eventually she was at the bottom. Laura helped her to her feet, picked her up and put her on the settee in front of the fire.

"You're a very brave little girl, our Emma. Did you know that?" Polly smiled in admiration.

"That's what my dad says, but it's not too bad. I hope I'll be able to walk soon. Eddie has been in to see me and he says he will help me in the summer."

Polly smiled her encouragement and then followed Laura into the kitchen, closing the door behind her while Emma picked up her book of nursery rhymes.

"How have you been, Laura?" Polly asked hesitantly, trying to judge from her sister's expression what was going on behind the façade of her smile.

"I've been alright, and it's so good to have Emma home again. She seems quite bright doesn't she?"

"Considering what she's been through, I was relieved to see how normal she seems. How's George taking it?"

"Well, you know how he is. He's taken against you and Chris but at least we can see each other again. I've really missed you, Polly." Tears threatened to spill so Laura turned away and started to get cups and saucers out of the cupboard.

"I've got some news too, Laura. I'm expecting. Can you believe it after all this time?"

Laura turned around in surprise, "Oh, Polly. I'm so happy for you both. When did you find out?"

"Last week. It must have happened either in December or January because the doctor says I'm three months. I'd been worrying about Emma so much I hadn't noticed I missed. It was only when Mrs Garside commented on my weight that I realised."

When the tea was made they settled themselves in the living room with Emma and talked generally. Polly noticed a certain reluctance in Laura to talk about George, but put it down to the fact that she felt awkward about his attitude towards her and Chris. They laughed and giggled together like old times and the time sped by. Emma was delighted to hear she was going to have another cousin to play with and asked Laura to teach her how to knit.

"I'm going to have to starting knitting, I suppose," Polly said.

"Don't sound so cheerful about it," Laura replied, laughing.

"I hate knitting and sewing, you know I do. Can you remember when you used to alter mam's clothes for us to wear before the war. I remember you made a pair of curtains into a lovely dress for yourself. Have you ever thought about doing that sort of thing again?

"No, not really. I've always gone out to work, but I suppose it's an idea. I could do alterations for people from home, couldn't I?" Polly could see she had planted a seed in Laura's mind.

"As long as you don't ask me to help. I'm useless at sewing. I can't even thread a needle without it getting knotted up."

Emma laughed, "Oh, Aunt Polly. You are silly. I bet you *can* thread a needle, even *I* can do that." She giggled into her hands and they all joined in.

Before she knew it, it was time for Polly to leave. She looked up at the sky as she stepped out of the back door. "It looks like rain, doesn't it? I hope I can get home before it starts. I didn't bring an umbrella."

"I'd lend you mine, but it's got more holes in it than enough. It would let more rain through than it stopped."

"Never mind, I'll just have to make a dash for it."

"I'll come again soon, Laura."

The sisters hugged each other and then Emma held out her arms for a hug and Polly was only too happy to oblige.

"Make sure you do."

***

Polly had made it as far as Holydyke when the heavens opened. She stepped into the doorway of the Holy Trinity Methodist Church to take shelter for a while. Her jacket was wet through and she cursed herself for being a vain fool in trying to look nice instead of dressing for the weather. Her ankle-high, kitten heel boots had rabbit fur around the tops which had seemed very elegant when she had looked in the mirror that morning now appeared bedraggled and ruined. The rain eased slightly but the sky still looked threatening when she decided to make another dash for home. There were very few people about as she hurried along towards the Market Place. Suddenly she heard a shout which made her turn awkwardly to see who it was. Her right foot slid beneath her and she fell into the road, directly into the path of a bullock which had escaped on its way to the slaughter house in Cottage Lane. Mr Hoodless came charging along the street. The last thing she heard before she fainted was the snort of the beast as it approached at full pelt. With great skill and courage, Frank put himself between Polly and the bullock, his arms stretched out wide causing it to veer to the right and suddenly stop. It lowered its head as if to charge, its breath snorting loudly as it pawed the ground. Mr Hoodless brought all his experience to the fore talking calmly to the animal all the time, and using a stick with a hook on the end, slipped it into the ring attached to the bullock's nose and led it calmly to the byre behind Holydyke.

Frank approached Polly, saw that she wasn't moving, and feared that she had died from fright. He was unsure what to do next when a car pulled up and Chris emerged, his face white with dread. He had called at home as usual for his lunch break and when he saw the rain, had decided to go to Laura's house to pick his wife up. He had arrived too late to meet her and had taken three different routes home before finding her.

"What's happened?" he gasped.

"She fell off kerb when beast frightened her, but it didn't touch her. She's alright isn't she?"

Chris picked Polly up and placed her in the back of the car. "I'm her husband. I'll get her home and call the doctor."

"Aye, that would be best. I hope she's alright though. I used to go to school with Polly, she's a right good lass."

"Thanks." Chris prayed with every ounce of his being that both she and the baby would be alright, but first things first - he would have to get her home.

Polly woke up to find herself tucked up in bed with Dr Birtwhistle listening to her heartbeat through his stethoscope. She looked around her neat bedroom and wondered how she had got there, but when she felt a pain in her ankle the memory of the morning's events came flooding back. Her stomach and back ached too and she instinctively put her hand over her abdomen and looked up at the doctor.

"Is the baby alright, Doctor?"

"It's a little early to tell, Polly." The answer came from Chris who was sat at the other side of the bed. She turned her head to see him looking pale-faced and anxious and then looked back at the doctor as he moved away to get a thermometer out of his bag.

"You've had a small amount of bleeding, Mrs Beauchamp. I don't think it's anything to worry about but you will need bed rest for a few days," he said calmly as he put the thermometer into her mouth.

Polly gripped Chris's hand and began to cry. The doctor tried to calm her, "Don't upset yourself, Mrs Beauchamp. It won't do the baby any good if you start crying. Be brave and all will be well, you'll see."

"We've waited so long for a baby, doctor. I don't want to lose it now."

"I really don't think it'll come to that – just try and keep calm and stay in bed for a few days. If the bleeding continues then we will have to send you to hospital, but let's not jump the gun, eh?"

As soon as Chris had shown the doctor out he went into the kitchen to reassure Mrs Garside and to make a cup of tea for Polly.

"She's got to stay in bed, so you'll have to make sure she does, Mrs Garside."

"Don't you worry, Master Chris. I'll make sure she doesn't move a muscle for at least three days."

"I wish you would drop the 'master' bit, Mrs Garside. It's a bit old fashioned now wouldn't you say?"

NINE

Laura and George sat opposite each other by the fireside that evening and as he buried his face behind the newspaper she wondered when it was that she had stopped loving him. The realisation stabbed at her heart as she faced the truth of the matter, and she pondered on how they would get through life together if her feelings became apparent. So far, he hadn't commented on the distance that had grown between them but she wondered if he had noticed. Did he feel the same? The question hung in her mind as he rustled the paper and turned to the sports page. It seemed that the joy they had once found in each other's company had melted away and their previous intimacy had never been fully restored since he had returned from Burma. Guilt flooded her as she considered how much George had lost to the war, or rather, what they had both lost. In effect, she had lost the man she had married and a stranger had returned in his place.

She stared into the fire remembering times past, smiling at some of the recollections but feeling unable to share them with George. He laughed very rarely nowadays, deep lines etched the sides of his mouth, and his temper was nearly always close to the surface, except where Emma was concerned. His love for his daughter was never in question, but Laura felt unable to reach out to him any longer, and because of his illnesses, bedtime was always just that – a place to sleep. They no longer shared giggles and joy under the sheets as they used to and their marriage was suffering greatly as a result.

The sudden banging on the back door startled her from her reverie and she stood up to go and answer it. She was amazed to find Chris standing on the threshold looking apologetic.

"I'm sorry for taking you unawares Laura, but I thought you might like to know that Polly has had an accident."

At his words the colour drained from Laura's face and she moved back into the kitchen, motioning for him to come in. "Is she alright?"

"She's in bed, resting. The doctor says she mustn't get up for a few days but she wanted me to let you know what happened."

Laura held open the living room door and entered first, holding it open for Chris to follow her. George looked up and without waiting for an explanation his temper exploded.

"I thought I told you that you weren't welcome here when I'm at home. What do you think you're doing marching in here at this time of night?"

"I'm sorry, George, but…"

"I don't want any of your excuses. You're not welcome. I've told you before we don't want your charity."

Laura tried to intervene, "George, he's come to tell us about Polly. She's had……"

"I don't want to know about Polly, you only saw her this morning. Now if you don't mind, Mr Beauchamp, I'd rather you left."

Chris retreated sheepishly into the kitchen followed by Laura.

"I'm so sorry, Chris. He blows his top at the least thing these days. Tell me what happened to Polly."

Chris related the events of the afternoon to Laura who stood wide-eyed as she listened. She put her hand over her mouth when he mentioned the charging bullock and her imagination ran riot. "She is alright though isn't she? It didn't trample her or anything?"

"No, she's alright, thanks to Mr Hoodless and Frank. I turned up just as they had caught the beast and led it away. It must have known it was going to the abattoir."

"There's always one gets away. I've lost count of the number of times I've seen men chasing them around the town. I'll try and get to see her some time this week. Tell her I'm thinking of her."

Suddenly Laura remembered the baby, "Oh, Chris. What must you think of me? Is the baby alright, she hasn't lost it has she?"

Chris saw how anxious she was and hurried to reassure her that hopefully all would be well. He took his leave and Laura returned to the living room.

"How could you be so rude, George?"

"This is my house and I......."

"Now you listen to me," Laura hissed through her teeth. "Polly is my sister and Chris came round to tell me she has had an accident, but would you listen? Oh no, not you. You and your stupid prejudices. I'm really sick and tired of listening to you and your daft ideas about this, that and the other."

George moved uncomfortably in his chair and picked up the newspaper again. "Well how was I supposed to know what had happened?"

Laura gasped at his words, "If you'd given Chris the time to speak instead of coming the big 'I am' you'd have heard what he had to say. She might lose her baby after this and you sit there reading a newspaper."

George looked flint-eyed at his wife, "Maybe they'll realise how we felt when Emma was taken ill then."

"What! You mean-minded so and so. I never thought I'd say this, George, but I'm ashamed of you at times. I've put up with this for long enough and from now on I'll see Polly when I like, not just when you say so."

"I've told you she can come round here as long as I'm not in," George parried.

"Well, isn't that big of you." Laura was so infuriated she was past caring how he reacted.

"Don't come it with me, Laura. I'm the master in this house and you'll do as you're told."

"We'll see about that."

The conversation ended when she stormed out and went upstairs. Her heart was beating so quickly she felt faint. After looking in to make sure they hadn't woken Emma, she decided to have an early night. It was only eight-thirty but she would rather be alone in her bed than downstairs with George. How could she possibly feel the same about him when he acted so unreasonably? Again, her thoughts returned to earlier in the evening when she had been mulling things over. Surely, things couldn't go on like this. There had to be some light at the end of the tunnel, but somehow she wasn't optimistic.

Alone in her room, Emma turned to face the wall, tears running silently down her face. She had heard her uncle Chris knock at the door and her father's words, but her youth prevented her from understanding his torment. She had feigned sleep when her mother had looked in, knowing instinctively that she mustn't let them know she had heard anything. The adult world seemed a very difficult place for six year old to witness and knots tightened in her little stomach as she thought about her aunt Polly's accident and that she might lose the little baby that they had been so excited about earlier in the day. Thankfully, her pillow stifled the sobs that escaped her.

Laura too feigned sleep when George retired about an hour later. He had an early start the following morning but the pains in his chest weren't boding well for a good night's sleep. His row with Laura played on his mind and if he hadn't felt so unwell he would probably have reached for her and they could have comforted each other, but instead, he slid into the bed and turned his back to her. They both stared silently into the darkness.

***

Chris didn't tell Polly about his reception at the Taylor household or of George's attitude. He just told her that Laura would see her as soon as possible and to try not to worry. In fact, Chris was quite worried about George. The furrowed lines on his face evidenced his ill health. Instead of being offended by George's attitude, he was deeply concerned not only about his physical health but his mental state too. In the three months or so since they had met, George seemed to have aged ten years. Laura too was showing the strain of living with the worry, her skin was sallow and she had lost more weight. When he had first met her she had been a pretty girl, not on a par with his Polly of course, but nonetheless attractive. He felt saddened that her life had been difficult, first of all having to cope with Sean O'Connell and his bigamy, then finding happiness with George only having it all fall apart during the war – and then, of course, there was Emma. His heart contracted painfully when he thought of how that little girl had contracted polio. He didn't need George's accusations, he felt the guilt like a millstone around his neck, but dwelling on it wouldn't make it right, he knew that, and for Polly's sake he would have to try and live with it.

TEN

There was a mini heat wave between late May and early June when temperatures reached into the 90s. Polly was five months pregnant and the worry of losing her baby had finally abated. Her swollen stomach was a source of pride and she constantly moved her hands over the mound as if caressing the unborn child.

Laura had been able to bring Emma along to see her and Lucky, as she had named the kitten, in a rickety wheelchair which had been given to her by the Gilfoye family who owned a large house behind their own. Emma had grown stronger by alternately being pushed and then by leaning on it and pushing the chair itself. Her callipered leg swung out to the side as she walked a few steps and her left leg had grown stronger, acquiring a little more flesh over the months of exercise.

They had agreed to meet Polly in Baysgarth Park one Sunday to have a picnic and listen to the town band playing on the bandstand. Emma had been so excited to hear about the outing and had been looking forward to it all week. The weather had held and it promised to be another scorching hot day. George had declined the invitation to join them saying that he would go and visit his parents on Ramsden Avenue for a while. Polly and Mrs Garside had made some sandwiches for them all and had packed everything into a wicker hamper which she had found in the basement, an obvious relic from the Beauchamp's past. It was too heavy for her to carry alone so she borrowed Jim, the newly appointed gardener, to help take it across the road to the park. Jim was the son of the old gardener, Ned, and only recently had returned to Barton after finishing his tour of duty with the army in Berlin before being demobbed.

Laura and Emma were waiting beneath a horse chestnut tree which cast a canopy of shadow for them to shelter beneath. Emma was sitting on a plaid blanket, her callipered leg hidden beneath a long summer dress. She spied Polly walking with Jim and raised her hand to wave to them.

"Aunty Polly, we're over here," she cried and Laura went across to help relieve Jim of the basket.

"Shall I come back to help later, Mrs Beauchamp?" he asked politely.

"No, I think we'll be able to manage it once the food and drink have gone. Thanks Jim."

The park was quite full and people sat around enjoying the sunshine in their colourful summer clothes and listening to the band playing. In the distance children played on the swings and slide and Emma looked enviously on, wishing she could get up and play too. Polly noticed the wistful looks she cast in the direction of the playground.

"Do you want to go on the swings, Emma? We can go over if you want to."

"Not yet, Aunty Polly. Can we have a sandwich first? I'm staaarving!" she exaggerated, making Polly laugh. Emma joined in and before she knew it, Laura was laughing too, for the first time in months and months.

"Mrs Garside has packed us up a feast. We've even got some homemade ginger beer, so don't you go getting drunk our Emma," she smiled, making Emma laugh again.

The happy trio ate their sandwiches in contented accord, Emma making faces of ecstasy as she tucked into the food. Her delight knew no bounds when a jelly appeared and she wobbled it on her spoon as it approached her mouth. "Mmmmm. This is the best jelly I've ever tasted."

"It's the *only* jelly you've tasted lately," Laura added.

"Well it has to be the best then, doesn't it?" Emma replied cheekily.

"She's got you there, Laura." Polly pointed out.

As the picnic came to an end and the ginger beer bottles were emptied, Polly began packing the dishes away into the hamper. Eventually, they leaned back against the tree and Laura felt totally at peace as the sun dappled her face through the leaves. Polly watched as her sister's face lost some of the strain of the past few months and wished she could do something to help. Laura hadn't mentioned George for weeks, and whenever Polly tried to enquire after him, she always managed to change the subject.

"Look mam. There's Eddie and Douglas. I didn't think they would be here today." Emma waved at her friends and they turned from the path and made their way over to see her.

"Do you want to come to the swings with us, Emma?"

Laura looked startled and began to make excuses, "We've only just eaten, lads. We might have some ginger beer left if you want some. You can play with Emma here, can't you?"

The two boys knelt down on the blanket and Polly re-opened the hamper and handed them two old bottles with marble stoppers. "Cor, thanks Missus. This is lovely, in't it Doug?"

"Sure is," Douglas drained his cup, eyeing a couple of leftover sandwiches. Polly noticed his lingering gaze and couldn't resist offering them the last of the food, which didn't remain in the basket for long after that.

"Can Emma come now, Mrs Taylor?" Eddie asked.

Laura was still reluctant to entrust Emma to anyone, but the pleading in the little girl's eyes was something she couldn't deny.

"Alright, but be careful with her. Hold her hands both of you and don't leave her for one minute."

"We won't, don't worry."

Laura watched her daughter's ungainly departure and Polly studied her sister.

"Are you alright, our Laura? You don't seem to be your usual self."

Laura was taken off-guard by the question and tried to answer nonchalantly but the words stuck in her throat somehow. She leaned back against the tree and sighed heavily.

"Never could keep much from you, could I?"

"No. So spill the beans and tell me what's up. Is it George?"

Laura's face blanched. "Is it so obvious?"

"Not to somebody else maybe, but I know you and I can see something's wrong."

"Oh, Polly." Laura put her hands over her eyes for a moment before continuing, "I don't think I love him anymore and it's tearing me apart. I don't know what to do."

"Is it because of me? Because if it is I want you to forget about it and let it go. We're fine as we are and I don't mind that he doesn't want to see me and Chris anymore as long as I can still see you and Emma."

Large tears rolled unheeded down Laura's face but she continued as if in a trance. "I don't know when I first realised it. It was probably when Emma was taken ill and he started to show his real feelings. I don't recognise him as my husband, Polly. He's not the man I married. Do you remember before the war when we lived on Beck Hill, he was always so kind and generous? Well he's nothing like that anymore. We just live together as if we were brother and sister. There's nothing between us now."

Polly handed Laura a handkerchief which she took and wiped her eyes and blew her nose. "What am I going to do? Emma loves her dad and he loves her, although he's so stubborn I know it upsets her that he won't speak to you or Chris."

"I think you need a rest, Laura. It can't have been easy for either of you over the last six months, what with Emma and all. Maybe when you get your new house it will brighten things up a bit for you. You know, give you something to look forward to."

"I hope so, Polly. Truly I do."

Looking up towards the park entrance, giving Laura time to pull herself together, Polly was dismayed to see George marching towards them. "Look out, Laura. He's here. Did you say you would meet him?"

"No. I thought we were meeting back at his mam and dad's house later on."

Seconds later, Polly witnessed the change in George as he stood next to them and totally ignored her.

"Laura, where's Emma? Surely you haven't let her go off with anybody."

"Hello, George. No she's just over by the swings playing with the Baxter boys. She...."

"You've let her go off without you? What are you thinking of? She needs one of us with her all the time, I've told you that often enough."

He turned on his heels and went over to where Emma was being pushed on a swing by Douglas Baxter. They watched as George caught the swing and lifted Emma off it and carried her back to her mother, giving black looks to the boys and muttering under his breath. Emma was protesting that she wanted to stay and play but George was having none of it. He placed her gently in the old wheelchair and when the breeze tugged at Emma's dress, Polly noticed the sore places on her legs where the callipers had rubbed.

"Are your legs sore, Emma?" she asked innocently.

"They do rub a bit, Aunty Polly, but I was enjoying the swings. Douglas and Eddie say that they are going to help me walk properly again soon."

"That'll be lovely, Emma. Won't it George?"

This was the first time Polly had ventured a question to her brother-in-law, hoping that he would acknowledge her, but instead he scowled at Laura.

"Come on, we're going now. I'll push Emma for a while. Our Len's at mam's and he wants to tell us about the new houses. Our Ev is there with the new baby."

He walked away without glancing at either of the women and Laura shrugged her shoulders at Polly who grimaced in return.

"I'm sorry, Polly. What're you going to do about the picnic hamper? You can't carry it alone in your condition."

"Don't worry. I'll get Douglas and Eddie to carry it between them. I'll promise them some more ginger beer."

116

Polly smiled when Laura hugged her goodbye. "Don't worry, Laura. Things have a way of working themselves out."

She stood for some time watching George and Laura walk out of the park. She shook her head in silent despair at the thought of her sister's torment and wished as hard as she could that Laura might find happiness again. Then, decisively, she turned and waved to the two boys who seemed to have taken a special interest in Emma, and they were only too pleased to help carry the hamper back to The Elms for a reward of a penny each and more ginger beer.

It wasn't far to walk but the boys had to change hands a few times as the wicker was old and brittle on their fingers. She had the surprise of her life when Martin met her at the bottom of the steps and relieved the boys of their burden.

"Martin! I didn't know you were coming back. Is Antoinette with you?"

"No. Wait till we get inside and I'll explain everything."

Eddie knew where the kitchen door was and ran on ahead with Douglas in tow. Mrs Garside was on hand to pour more ginger beer for them and gave them a few sandwiches each which they ate with gusto, both of them eyeing a sponge cake, a piece of which they hoped might also come their way.

Martin thanked the boys for helping Polly with a penny each and they reluctantly left with a piece of cake clutched in sticky fingers, which they'd finished before reaching the bottom of the steps on Whitecross Street.

"It's good to see you both again," Martin repeated when they were all sitting in the living room.

Polly was sitting with her feet up on the sofa as her ankles had started to swell with the heat and Martin and Chris had the two fireside chairs. The windows were open to let in some air and an ancient fan was trying its best to waft the air around the room.

"Don't keep us in suspense, Martin. Did Antoinette find her mother?" Polly said impatiently.

Martin laughed, "In short, yes she did, but she got more than she bargained for. We made enquiries at the French Embassy and also with the Red Cross and the records showed her mother had found her way to England as we suspected, but she has since remarried and is planning to take her English husband with her back to the family home."

"Oh dear. How did Antoinette feel about that?"

"She didn't take it too well as you might expect. Her father's memory is still vivid in her mind and to have an Englishman as a step-father didn't go down very well at all."

"Is that why you've come back? Aren't you seeing her anymore?"

"I never was 'seeing her' in the sense you mean. You just took it for granted that I was and I couldn't be bothered to explain at Christmas or it might have complicated matters. I was ordered to accompany her as a thank you for all her help during the war. She is a very brave woman and I admire her, but that's as far as it goes."

"Are we never going to get you married off, Martin?" Chris asked.

"You've got the prettiest wife in the country, Chris, so anyone I met would only be second best. I'm not the marrying sort, you know that."

"Why, thank you brother-in-law," Polly smiled and threw a cushion in his direction, "now I know you must be after something. Come on – spit it out."

"Nothing. I'm not after anything at all," Martin rejoined.

Chris looked doubtful too, but said nothing.

"How's Laura and George these days?"

"I wish I could say she was blissfully happy, but she isn't. The war has changed George completely and since Emma's accident he has become withdrawn and refuses to speak to either me or Chris, no matter how much we try to apologise or make amends. He's only recently allowed Laura to have any contact with us."

Martin frowned and decided to change the subject.

"I haven't told you my main news, have I?"

"What main news?"

"I'm leaving the army and coming back home," he announced, looking at their dumb-struck faces with pleasure.

"I don't believe it," Chris said incredulously.

"Me neither. When is this going to happen, and come to that, why is it going to happen?" Polly added.

"I'm going to take up where father left off and get involved in politics. I thought maybe I could get onto the local Council and who knows where I'll end up."

"That's a brilliant idea, Martin. I can just imagine you as Mayor of Barton."

"Well, let's just see what happens shall we. I'm due a spot of leave, and then I'll be leaving the army at the end of it. I'll make some enquiries through father's old contacts and see how the land lies."

"That's really great news, Martin. Wait till I tell our Laura, she'll be pleased to hear your back to stay.

She's had a soft spot for you since you helped save me from that horrible Jane woman."

Martin looked embarrassed at her words and began fidgeting uncomfortably but was saved from further discomfort when Mrs Garside brought in the tea things.

ELEVEN

The next opportunity for Polly and Laura to meet up was at the Town Carnival which was held, for once, in perfect weather. The parade during the morning had travelled the main streets and terminated in Baysgarth Park where marquees had been set up, with bunting flying between each one. The colourful scene was reminiscent of pre-war days and lifted everyone's spirits.

The Carnival Queen had been crowned and children ran from place to place, trying to find a vantage point to see everything that was going on. Vegetables were being exhibited in one marquee, a Bonny Baby competition in another, whilst refreshments were disappearing fast. Polly caught sight of Laura and George standing together watching a children's sack race. Emma was in her chair clapping as Eddie jumped as fast he could to the finish line, falling through the tape with great drama. Laura was wearing a yellow polka-dot dress with a square neckline and low-heeled white shoes. Since George had been working, Laura had put on a little weight and looked a hundred times better than she had at Christmas. Emma looked a picture in a lavender sleeveless dress.

Chris and Martin disappeared into the beer tent and this gave Polly her chance to see how Laura was faring.

She went to stand next to her sister and Laura gave a start when she saw her.

"Oh, our Polly - you frightened me to death!" she breathed.

"Sorry, but I wanted to surprise you. You look nice, Laura. Hello George."

George ignored her as she knew he would but Emma held out her arms to her and she bent down to hug her.

"Hello my beautiful girl. How are you? I haven't seen much of you since our picnic. I like your dress, it really suits you."

"I'm alright, Aunty Polly," she answered unconvincingly. "Mam made our dresses; she's very clever, isn't she? Is Uncle Chris with you?"

"Yes, he's in the beer tent with Uncle Martin."

"Oh, Martin's back is he?" Laura seemed surprised.

Polly filled her in on the family's comings and goings over the past few weeks.

"Can we go and see them?" Emma asked innocently.

"You're not allowed in the beer tent," George stated bluntly.

"I'll bring her over, Polly, and we'll wait outside for them." Laura answered without waiting for George's approval.

He shrugged his shoulders saying he was going for a walk around the field.

Laura started to wheel Emma's chair towards the tents.

"Can I get out now, mam?" she asked.

"Alright, be quick then," Laura looked over her shoulder as she spoke but George was striding away with his hands in his pockets.

Polly noticed that Emma didn't have her calliper on but said nothing further, watching as she made a swift exit from the chair. They walked over to the beer tent and Polly was amazed at how steady Emma was on her legs. Her movement, although still a little ungainly, was much improved since the last time she had seen her. Mother and daughter waited outside the beer tent while Polly went in to find her husband and Martin. There was quite a crush with most of the male population of Barton trying to buy a pint of beer. Tables and chairs were set around the perimeter and these were mostly occupied by the ladies, with the men mingling around the makeshift bar, Chris and Martin being two of them.

When Polly explained that Laura and Emma were outside they pushed their way through the huddle to where they were standing. Martin was obviously pleased to see them again after so long, giving Laura a brief peck on the cheek and picking Emma up to hug her. Emma was a little unsure of this as she hadn't seen him much, except at Christmas, and he was almost a stranger to her, but she soon settled in his arms and put her arm around his neck.

"Well now Miss. I understand you've been a bit poorly since I last saw you," he said, tweaking her nose.

Emma laughed and nodded shyly. "But I'm a lot better now, Uncle Martin."

"Let's see how you can walk then."

He put her down on the grass and she paraded up and down, limping slightly still, but so much improved.

"You've done really well, haven't you?" Chris said, extremely pleased and relieved that she had recovered so well.

"The doctor says I needn't sit in the chair, but dad says I have to or I might fall. I won't though, will I, mam?"

Polly looked towards Laura who rolled her eyes at Emma's statement. Again, nothing further was said but a mental note was made by Polly to get to the bottom of things with her sister.

"Shall we take Emma to the swings, Laura?"

"Yes alright. It looks like George has gone off in a sulk again. He'll turn up eventually I suppose."

"Are you staying for the dance in the evening, Laura?" Martin asked.

"I'll have to check with George," she replied as she walked away.

The men disappeared back into the tent as the women headed towards the swings.

The Saturday night dance was a carnival tradition and everyone looked forward to it. The long years of the war had deprived the townspeople of many social events but everyone was looking forward to a new era of peace. Food was still on ration but every week more and more things were being made available in the shops.

Once they reached the playground, Emma decided she wanted to sit on the rocking horse. It had had a new coat of varnish for the carnival and looked quite smart, but being box-shaped Emma found it a little difficult to sit comfortably but she was insistent that she did it herself. Laura and Polly strolled away to an empty bench and sat down, watching while Emma struggled to put her leg over the horse which she eventually managed and laughed as other children joined her.

"What's been happening then, Laura?" Polly wasted no time in pumping her sister for information.

"We've had a letter from the Council and we'll be moving into one of the new houses on Bowmandale in a couple of months. I can't wait to have my own washhouse and toilet again."

"That's really good news. Is George happy about it?"

"I think so. I'm hoping he'll be able to settle there. Len is just up the road on Providence Crescent, and his mam and dad are only up Ramsden. I hope they can cheer him up a bit."

"Are things any better since I last saw you?"

"No, not really." Laura stared off into the distance as if lost in her thoughts.

"Emma seems a lot better though."

"She's done well with her exercises and is determined to make a complete recovery. Now that she can walk reasonably well, she's going back to school in September. I think she's looking forward to that."

"It'll do her good to get among her friends again."

"I hope so. George of course is still trying to wrap her in cotton wool, but she's refused to wear her calliper since the picnic. Her leg was getting so sore it was making her limp even more."

"It's just as well she's determined then. Why do you think he wants to mollycoddle her? You'd think he'd want her to get better as quickly as possible."

"I don't know. It's as if he wants her to be dependent on him. I'm really quite worried about him, Polly. He loses his temper so much these days and mostly for no reason at all. He gets a lot of migraine headaches but I think it's all self-inflicted. If he would only relax a bit instead of forever picking fault with everything, he might not get so many."

"Let's hope things will improve when you move. You will let me know when that's happening, won't you? Will he let me help you, do you think?"

"I doubt it. He's hoping to borrow a cart or lorry from somebody he knows, but I'm not sure. I'll let you know though."

Emma began to dismount from the horse and had just about made it when George thundered up to her and grabbed her round her waist.

"What do you think you're doing? You know you'll fall." He looked over to where Laura and Polly were sitting and Polly felt her sister tense.

"Dad, leave me alone, I can do it." Emma was screaming and kicking her legs until he put her down. She moved awkwardly round to look at her father, her distress evident. "I can manage, dad, really I can," she implored, almost begging him to understand.

George was surprised at Emma's reaction and looked daggers at Laura who was walking towards him. "You should be looking after her, not sat gassing with your sister. That's how all this happened in the first place," he shouted.

"There's no need to shout, George. Emma likes to manage on her own, it makes her stronger – can't you see that?"

He was about to answer when his face turned grey and he put his hands to his head. "Blast these migraines. I'm off home, Laura. You can do as you like."

"I will, don't you worry."

He turned on his heels and stormed out of the park gates without looking back.

"I suppose we'll have to go after him, Polly. Sorry for spoiling the afternoon for you."

"You haven't spoiled the afternoon. I tell you what – you wait here and I'll get Martin to give you all a lift home. You can pick George up on the way. Maybe he'll be alright later and you can come back for the dance."

Laura nodded and sat down with Emma on the bench while Polly went in search of the men. When Martin heard of what had transpired he ran over to Laura and picked Emma up. "Come on, I'll get the car out and take you home. It's too far for you to walk and George won't feel like walking if he's unwell."

They caught up with George on the High Street and after his initial reluctance to accept any form of help he was persuaded to get into the car. Martin was amazed at the difference in him but kept his anxieties to himself until he could speak to Polly and Chris.

There was an attempt at desultory conversation but Martin found it hard going to keep it up, so lapsed into silence until they reached Humber Terrace. There was nobody much around as nearly all the population was at the carnival. George got out of the car and made his way into the house leaving Laura and Emma to help get the wheelchair out of the boot which had been tied with string to stop it falling out. Martin was appalled at George's lack of manners and would have accompanied them into the house but Laura forestalled him.

"You've been very kind, Martin, and thank you for bringing us home, but we can manage ourselves now. If George is feeling better later we might come back for the dance, but the way things are looking, it's not likely. But thanks again."

"Only too happy to help, Laura, and if you need me just let me know."

Laura almost wept at his thoughtfulness but ushered Emma inside and closed the door.

"If you need me, just let me know," George mimicked as she made her way through to the living room.

"Put a sock in it, George. He was only being helpful."

"If I didn't feel so bad, I'd tell him where to stick his help."

Emma started crying at their words and went to her room as quickly as she could, slamming the door behind her.

"You've upset Emma again now. Why don't you think before you open your mouth? I'm going up to her."

George gave her an unrepentant stare and started to fill the kettle for a cup of tea. The pain behind his eyes was excruciating and he bent forward just in time to vomit into the sink. He held onto the edge of the porcelain with white fingers as he fought the urge to faint. He ran the tap to wash away the evidence and stood erect just before Laura came down the stairs.

"Emma's having a sleep," she said shortly and moved to the cupboard to prepare the cups and saucers for the tea. George said nothing and she looked at him out of the corner of her eye, noting his pallor. Anxiety returned knotting her stomach in the process.

"Go and sit down, George. I'll bring you a cup of tea."

Again he said nothing but went obediently into the living room and drew the curtains to keep out the bright sun which made his headaches worse. Laura found him with his eyes closed slumped in his chair and placed his tea on the mantelpiece where he could reach it without knocking it over. She noticed his hands trembled as he reached for the cup.

"I wish you would see the doctor again, George. It can't be right that you're having so many migraines lately."

"I'll call in next week when I get home from work and see if he can suggest anything."

"Drink your tea and then go and have a lie down. You might feel better later and we can go to the dance. Dot Baxter's already said she'll come round and sit with Emma if we want to go."

George turned his head to look at her and for once tried to understand her need for company. He had been useless as a husband since returning from Burma. The sights he had seen there had come back to haunt him in his nightmares, rendering him impotent. He wouldn't admit to this of course, but seeing her and Emma in their new dresses, which Laura had made herself especially for the carnival, made him realise how selfish he had been. He smiled a rare smile saying, "Why don't you go anyway. I'll stay here with Emma. I'm sure Polly will bring you back afterwards."

"I don't want to go without you, George. It won't be the same."

"I'm going up for a sleep. Come and tell me when you're going and I'll get up and sit with Emma until her bedtime."

"I'll think about it," she replied uncertainly.

George lay in his bed thinking, remembering, wishing and dreading. He knew things were going from bad to worse in his marriage but felt unable to stop it. How he managed to find the strength to continue working he didn't know, he only knew he was grateful for the fact that he did. The sun was still shining behind the thin fabric of the curtains, throwing shadows into the room. He turned his back on it and closed his eyes. Somehow he must try to love Laura again – not that he didn't – he just couldn't show it.

He fell asleep and began dreaming again. He could smell the jungle around him; feel the tingling of sweat on his skin as he marched with his friends and colleagues, trees, broken branches and high grasses blocking their advance. They reached a swamp-like expanse of water, green with algae and felt the familiar dread as they were ordered to wade through it. Holding their rifles high as they did so, he felt the fine mud suck at his boots, heard the twitter of birds and the screech of animals in the trees overhead. Suddenly, there was a shot. They all dived for the far bank, scrambling out, eyes wide and searching for the sniper, but all they saw was young Alex Swann, a lad barely eighteen, lying face down in the water, blood seeping from a wound to his head, staining the water in pink ribbons. No-one moved for a second or two then George slipped back into the water and dragged the young boy back to join the rest of his unit. As he bent down to see if there was any sign of life in the lad's body, another shot cracked and a bullet whistled past his head and buried itself in the arm of Lieutenant Kitchen, his commanding officer.

They all ran into the cover of the jungle, dragging Alex's body behind them, the lieutenant gasping against the pain in his arm. They found a clearing and were just about to set up camp when all hell broke loose. Shots were being fired from all directions; a hail of bullets striking trees and men alike. George threw himself behind a fallen tree trunk just in time, as other men followed his example. Suddenly, the firing stopped. All was silent except for the groaning of the injured then he heard a twig snap behind him and the click of a rifle and felt cold steel against his head. He turned to find he was looking down the barrel of a gun and raised his eyes to see who was holding it. Gulping down the desire to scream he looked into the eyes of Martin Beauchamp. The face changed each time he had the dream, but it always ended the same way with him waking up, never knowing if the gun was fired.

The nightmare woke him again. Sweating and shaking he looked around the room trying to get his bearings. When he realised he was safely in bed he flopped down onto his pillows, breathing deeply to still his trembling body. Night after night he had been woken by scenes from the war, especially Burma. Reality had been one nightmare after another so why couldn't he just forget it now that he was at home? Depression permeated his soul once more and he closed his eyes and slept mercifully without dreaming.

***

Laura and Emma were in the living room when George stumbled down the stairs. It was seven thirty and although the sun had lowered in the sky, the heat of the day still lingered. Emma was sitting at a small table doing a jigsaw puzzle and Laura was sewing buttons onto one of his shirts.

"I thought you were going to wake me so that you could go to the dance with your Polly."

"I didn't like to. You seemed so tired earlier and it doesn't matter about the dance."

"Well, I think you ought to go. You don't get out much these days and it will do you good. Go and get ready and me and Emma will read a book till her bedtime."

"Yes, go on, mam. You'll have a lovely time," Emma interjected.

"Well if I'm not wanted, I might as well," Laura teased.

She went upstairs and changed into another dress which she had made from a remnant she had found in the market. It was pink with small white rose buds printed onto the fabric and it fitted her slim figure perfectly. She felt a million dollars in it. She creamed off the makeup she had been wearing during the day with Ponds cold cream and then put on a fresh layer of foundation and powder. The lipstick she had found in Lee's chemists at a sale price matched her dress and she realised she hadn't felt so light-hearted for many months. She tripped lightly down the stairs and presented herself for inspection.

"Wow, mam, is that really you? You look lovely," was Emma's comment.

George swallowed the threatened lump in his throat saying, "Have a nice time and be careful."

"Don't worry - Polly will bring me home." Looking at the clock she realised the time and after a quick kiss goodbye she ran out of the house.

TWELVE

Laura called at The Elms just as Polly, Chris and Martin were leaving. They were happy to see her and headed immediately for the large marquee in the park where the dance was being held. Polly was wearing a very loose blue dress with an inverted pleat down the front and the men were dressed casually in blazers and slacks. Martin held his blazer over his arm revealing the whitest of shirts and Laura thought he had never looked so handsome.

A dance band had just finished playing *Pennsylvania Six Five Thousand* and followed up with *In The Mood*, both Glenn Miller numbers, as they approached causing Laura and Polly to reminisce over the dances they used to attend at the Assembly Rooms and the Odd Fellows Hall before the war. An old generator hummed and clanked alternately as it provided electricity for the crowded tent, but the band was in full swing as they entered. The excitement of the music and the thrill of an evening out made Laura's heart race and her eyes were more brilliant than they had been for a very long time. A smile never left her lips and Martin leaned in closer to ask her if she wanted a drink.

"Just a lemonade please," she shouted in his ear. She noticed how good his cologne smelled and thought that George would never dream of wearing anything like that for fear of being called a sissy by his friends and family. She could never understand why most working-class men would buy perfume for their wives and girlfriends but were quite happy to smell terrible themselves.

Polly nudged her, "Look, there's a table over there, let's go and sit down for a while."

Although her baby wasn't due for about six weeks yet, Polly's ankles were prone to swell at the least excuse and the doctor had advised her to rest. This dance though, was one opportunity she was determined not to miss.

Chris and Martin returned with drinks and they sat for a while watching other couples dance. The band began to play *Moonlight Serenade* and Martin asked Laura if she would like to dance she looked unsure.

"Oh, go on, our Laura. You didn't come here to sit with me all night. Go and have a dance," was Polly's advice.

"Alright, then. Thanks, Martin."

They joined the swaying throng in the centre of the tent and once again she was very aware of his presence. He held her firmly as they were forced to dance very close together due to the crush. It had been a long time since anyone had held her, and Martin's military bearing and strong arms made her feel safe and secure. She steeled herself not to let him know how vulnerable she was, and kept reminding herself that George was waiting at home.

Martin, too, was thinking of George as he held Laura in his arms. Polly had hinted at Laura's unhappiness and his attraction to her was something he would have to keep under control, or he might lose her friendship. In no time it seemed the dance was over and they rejoined Chris and Polly at the table.

"It's a bit hectic out there Polly. If you decide to dance I suggest you wait till there's a bit more room."

"I don't think I'll be doing any dancing. Just look at my ankles already."

Laura looked down at her sister's puffy ankles and pulled a face.

"They look pretty bad, Polly. Are you okay?"

"I'm a bit tired but not too bad, thanks. We'll stay for a bit longer and then Chris will take me home. You stay with Martin though and enjoy yourself."

"I was hoping you might be able to run me home later. George was a bit poorly with a migraine this afternoon."

Martin stepped in, "Don't worry, Laura. I'll take you home."

"Well that's that sorted then," Polly smiled.

They relaxed and enjoyed each other's company, occasionally Martin and Laura would get up for another dance, but Polly was feeling the effects of walking around the field during the afternoon and an hour later she and Chris made ready to leave for home.

"Do you want me to come with you?" Laura asked, concerned that her sister looked so tired.

"No, I'm off to bed when I get home. I feel really tired. I think I might have overdone it this afternoon. You stay and enjoy yourself."

"I'll come up and bring Emma later on in the week then, shall I?

"I'd love to see you both." Polly leaned over and kissed Laura's cheek. Chris winked at her in his usual amiable way and put his arm round Polly as he led her off into the night."

"Do you want another dance, Laura?" Martin asked.

"Yes, I think I would," she replied, feeling carefree and young again.

"Come on then, this one's a bit livelier."

135

They were breathless when they emerged from the crowd five minutes later, laughing together after reliving old memories with a jitter bug.

"I think I must be getting old," Martin mused as he tried to get his breath.

"Me too," Laura agreed, "I'm a bit older than you I think."

"Well you don't look it, Laura my love. I think I'm going grey already," he laughed. "Shall we have a breath of air do you think?"

"I could do with it after that," she agreed.

They emerged from the marquee into a balmy, starlit night and began walking towards the tennis courts near Baysgarth House. They wandered slowly, arm in arm, enjoying the peace and quiet after the uproar of the marquee. Occasionally, they met other couples seeking solitude and Martin looked at Laura as they took the meandering path, bordered by trees on one side, past the old sundial and came out near to the bandstand. He had never seen her looking so lovely, her dress suited her to perfection and he was just about to compliment her on it when she interrupted his thoughts.

"What time is it, Martin?" Laura asked, not sure if she wanted to know or not.

He consulted his wristwatch, "It's only nine thirty. Do you need to be in at any particular time?"

"No, not really, but I don't want to be too late in case George is waiting up for me."

"I tell you what, then. Instead of taking the car, why don't I walk you back home? It's a long walk, I know, but we don't have to rush."

Laura felt her heart skip a beat and wondered at her emotions. How could a grown woman have these feelings? She was a wife and mother for goodness sake. She should have more sense.

Martin too was struggling inwardly with his own thoughts and feelings. He had known Laura for a long time and had always admired her, but the war had taken him away for years at a time. When he had seen her again at Christmas he had noticed a difference in her demeanour and her appearance. She had looked frail somehow which made him want to protect her, and when Polly had hinted at her unhappiness his chivalrous nature spurred him on to go and rescue her. He smiled to himself as he thought of galloping on a white horse, charging down Waterside to rescue the damsel in distress. But, of course, it was no laughing matter - he could feel her vulnerability and warned himself not to take advantage of it.

Laura studied him from under her lashes. He had changed little since Christmas except that perhaps his hair was streaked with a little more grey than before, but she thought it made him more handsome. He was only two years younger than she was so at thirty he would be a good catch for some lucky woman. She just managed to stop herself from sighing out loud.

"What are you thinking about?" Martin squeezed her hand to bring her back to the present.

"I was just thinking that this is the first time in years I've been out dancing," she lied.

"I wish I could take you out more often, Laura." Martin bit his lip as the words escaped. He hadn't intended to say that. What was the matter with him?

Laura was taken aback too, but she made light of it, "I don't think George would be very happy about that, do you?"

"Probably not, but would *you*?"   There he went again.   He really must take more care to keep his thoughts in check.

Laura was silent.   What could she say?   At that moment she stumbled on the kerb as they crossed the road to the High Street. Martin's arms were around her in a flash.   It had been pure reaction on his part to stop her from falling, but now that she was so close he couldn't resist holding her tightly against him.   He felt her breath on his neck and she breathed in the scent of his cologne; the mixture of sandalwood and spices sent her senses reeling and she wondered fleetingly how it would be to be kissed by him.   Realising how it would seem if someone happened upon them, she knew she ought to move away from him, but it just felt right somehow.   The thought must have crossed both their minds simultaneously as they parted awkwardly, but at the same time reluctantly.

"That was a close one," he said trying to lighten the situation.

She caught his drift and continued in the same vein, "I thought I was going to fall into the road.   Thanks for rescuing me."

He bowed with great exaggeration, "At your service, ma'am."

The tension of the moment was broken and they continued on their way.   Both were glad of the darkness as they cut down Queen Street to Butts Lane, both attempting to reel in their senses.

Twenty minutes later they were outside Humber Terrace and as the light was on in the living room,

Laura presumed George was still up. They stood outside on the pavement for a second while Laura reached up to peck Martin on the cheek.

"Thanks for seeing me home," she muttered briefly before turning quickly and hurrying inside.

The back door was unlocked and she stepped into the kitchen expecting to find George in the living room but when she opened the door she found Jenny Shooter from the end house sitting there.

"Hello, Jenny – where's George?" she asked, baffled to find George absent.

"He said he was going to the dance to find you."

"I never saw him. He'll be back later I suppose. Thanks for sitting with Emma."

"That's alright, Mrs Taylor. Mr Taylor gave me sixpence."

Jenny left and Laura went upstairs to check on Emma and satisfied herself that she was sleeping soundly and went to the kitchen to make a cup of tea.

***

Outside, Martin suddenly felt lonely and somehow disconnected from everything around him, so instead of heading back to The Elms he walked ahead to the place the locals called Point. He stood at the low- walled area and gazed out across the Humber. The tide was in and the brown, muddy waters lapped at the banks. The still warmth of the night and the stars twinkling in the blackness brought on a melancholy mood he had rarely experienced before, so he sat on the wall to consider his future.

When he had decided to leave the army at the end of his last tour in Berlin, he was looking forward to a future in politics, whether national or local, but now he wasn't sure. Perhaps he should contact the army again and ask to re-enlist. Yes, surely that's what he must do. It wasn't too late to change his mind; his commanding officer had been clear on that score. He could perhaps take up the posting to Hong Kong he had been offered – at least he would be far enough away from Laura to get some peace of mind.

Since Christmas she had peppered his thoughts and dreams. He had said nothing to anyone and Antoinette's presence had acted as a convenient camouflage at the time. Now though, he had no-one to hide behind and his love, yes love – he admitted it now to himself - for Laura was all consuming. He hadn't dared to admit it before, always moving from place to place he had managed to dodge his emotions, but now, if he stayed in Barton, he could not be so confident.

His thoughts were shattered abruptly, when he heard someone approaching from behind. Turning he saw George walking towards him but missed the scowl or he would have been more prepared.

"Now then, Beauchamp, enjoyed yourself with *my wife* tonight, have you?"

Martin was left in no doubt of George's mood now. He stood to face the irate husband who, although narrower in build, was almost as tall as him. The first punch landed squarely on Martin's chin, taking him by surprise, and which he admitted to himself, he probably deserved. Recovering from the punch, Martin felt blood trickle from a split lip at the corner of his mouth. He wiped it away with his left hand, holding out his right arm in a conciliatory gesture, attempting to calm the other man.

"We've only been dancing, George. She's at home waiting for you."

"Don't give me that. I saw you with my own eyes back there in the town. You were cuddling up to her, I saw you."

"No, you've got it wrong, George."

George was in no mood to listen to any explanations. His slighter build gave him the edge over his rival and he closed the gap between them once more and landed another punch on Martin's nose, causing it to bleed profusely.

"I don't want to hurt you, George, but I will if you don't stop this. Laura almost fell off the kerb and I caught her before she fell, that's all that happened. Ask her yourself." He pulled out his handkerchief and tried to stem the flow of blood from his nose.

"She'll just lie to me like you are. I'm not blind. I saw what was going on."

"No you didn't. You only saw part of it."

Martin was getting desperate now to calm him down. He knew that if he landed one punch in anger he might finish George off for good and Laura would never forgive him.

As if she knew his thoughts, Laura could be heard calling George's name. She had waited half an hour for him to return and then gone in search of him. Her anxiety was gnawing at her stomach when he couldn't be found so she had decided to walk up to Point to see if he was there. What she found was a bruised and bleeding Martin with George moving in for another punch.

"George, what on earth do you think you're doing? Martin! What are you still doing here?"

"Come to save your fancy man, have you?" George threw the accusation at her wildly.

"He's not my fancy man, George. Come back home, I've left Emma asleep on her own."

"I saw you both in the town. I *saw* you, Laura. Like I said to *him* – I'm not blind. I can see what's going on."

Laura looked desperately at Martin, torn between wanting to go to him to soothe his hurts and trying to calm George down enough to get him to listen to reason. Common sense took over and she went to George, holding his arm to restrain him from causing any further damage to her brother-in-law.

"George. Listen to me. I don't know what you think you saw but you've got it all wrong. Come back home now and we'll talk about it." She looked at Martin. "Go home, Martin. You look terrible."

George still wasn't sure but he could feel his chest starting to tighten and knew he ought to do as his wife suggested. Laura felt him relax slightly and knew she had won. She tightened her hold on his arm and moved him slowly back towards home.

Martin followed at a distance and she turned to look at him as she led George through the gate, hoping she could convey with one look how sorry she was. He caught the meaning and smiled into the moonlight, knowing in that moment that she felt the same way about him as he did about her. The pain from the punches receded as his heart soared, but his mind was made up. He would re-enlist.

THIRTEEN

The expression on Chris's face when he saw his brother in such a dishevelled state made Martin smile, splitting his lip again and causing him to wince as a fresh spurt of blood ran down his chin.

"What on earth have you been up to?" Chris asked as he went to help his brother.

"Fighting for a fair lady's reputation and honour," he replied jokingly.

"Who? What do you mean?"

"George's got it into his head that Laura and me are an item. She almost fell off the kerb as we crossed the road and I caught her. He was watching us and thinks something's going on. He landed a couple of lucky punches."

"Wait till Polly hears about this. She'll go mad. Thankfully though, she's fast asleep at the moment. Come on, I'll help you get cleaned up."

That wasn't the only drama to face the occupants of The Elms that night. Polly went into labour. She felt her back ache first and was woken by strong cramps in the pit of her abdomen. She shook Chris awake and explained what was happening. He immediately ran down the stairs and rang the doctor and the midwife who arrived almost simultaneously fifteen minutes later.

"Why do babies always choose the middle of the night to make an appearance?" Nurse Beswick bustled into the room and Polly smiled uncertainly and looked at Dr Birtwhistle for an answer.

Instead of answering he pulled back the sheet which was the only bed covering due to the humidity and started to examine Polly's tummy.

"Have the waters broken yet, Doctor?" the nurse asked as she wiped her freshly washed hands on a fluffy towel.

"No. I'm hoping this is a false labour. We don't want this baby to make an appearance too soon, do we Polly?"

Polly shook her head, not sure if she did or not. She had been so uncomfortable for days now and the baby seemed to have lowered in her abdomen.

"How far apart are the contractions?" the nurse asked.

"They're erratic and slowing down," the doctor answered.

"Does that mean I won't have the baby tonight after all?" Polly asked.

"Let's hope not. Premature babies can be at risk, so the longer you hold onto this one the better for all concerned."

"I do feel a bit easier now. I'm sorry if it's a false alarm but I panicked when I started getting pains."

"Every new mother gets frightened, Polly. No need to apologise. It's better to be safe than sorry. At least I can assure you that your baby is in the correct position so labour should be normal."

"Thank you, Doctor."

Martin hovered at the entrance to the room and Polly caught sight of his bruised face complete with sticking plaster on his nose and chin.

"Martin! What on earth has happened to you?"

"Nothing serious, Polly, I'll explain in the morning."

Polly took the hint not to ask any further questions but looked at Chris who shrugged his shoulders innocently.

When it was obvious that the baby would not be making an appearance, the doctor and midwife took their leave giving Chris instructions to keep Polly in bed for the next week. She was to have complete rest and was only allowed downstairs after that if she agreed to keep her feet up on the sofa. Chris assured her that he would make sure she did. Luckily, he was in the middle of the school holidays so had no work commitments at all, but even so, he knew Mrs Garside would insist Polly rested in his absence.

Back at Waterside, Laura had insisted that she and George should talk through their problems. Unfortunately, he wasn't very forthcoming and it was a one-sided conversation as far as she was concerned. She explained how she had fallen off the kerb and how Martin had caught her, but she could tell by his face that he wasn't convinced. In the end she gave it up as a bad job and decided to go to bed.

George followed reluctantly half an hour later. Laura had turned over to face the wall and he once more lay next to her not touching and more distant than ever.

He pondered the events of the evening. He had put Emma to bed around nine o'clock and then a bit later had decided a walk might lift his headache altogether. He saw young Jenny Shooter as she passed by the kitchen window and he approached her to babysit while he went to meet Laura from the dance. He played the scene he had witnessed over and over again in his mind, convinced he was in the right. They hadn't seen him, of course, he had ducked into a doorway and they had been so wrapped up in each other they hadn't noticed him watching. He hadn't bothered to follow them back but had taken an altogether different route home. An icy hand clutched at his heart and his thoughts brought on another headache. He got out of bed to get some aspirin hoping they might help him sleep.

"Are you alright, George?" Laura's voice echoed her concern.

"What do you care? I'm going to get some aspirin. I've got another headache coming on."

"Shall I get some for you?"

"No. I'll get them myself," he replied dismissively.

Laura heard him go down the stairs to the kitchen where she listened as he filled a glass and imagined him taking the tablets. He didn't immediately come back to bed and she guessed he would go into the living room for a while. She got out of bed and stood at the window looking out into the night sky lit by a full moon. When the faint strains of music from the wireless filtered through the floorboards she went back to bed realising he might be some time coming back. It was almost daybreak when she finally closed her eyes and slept and George still hadn't come back to bed.

George had slept fitfully on the sofa and struggled with his thoughts and feelings all night. He tried to be objective even though he found it difficult but having weighed up the evidence of his own eyes against the explanation given by Martin Beauchamp and Laura independently, he realised that he may have been slightly hasty. Not that he was sorry for punching Martin – he actually felt better having done so. It had dissolved the bad feeling he had harboured against the

Beauchamp family and he thought he should have hit him or Chris sooner. It might have saved him from having so many headaches. On reflection he knew that Laura wouldn't have been unfaithful to him and decided to give her the benefit of the doubt, but he would make her wait and suffer the way he had.

It was late Sunday morning when Laura woke to the sound of children chanting a rhyme to see who would be 'it' in their next game.

"Colman's mustard
Colman's starch
Colman's blue
And out goes you."

Then she heard irate mothers as they rounded up their children for Sunday school, threatening them with a fate worse than death if they messed up their Sunday best clothes.

She roused slowly, thinking through the events of the night before and wondered how Martin was feeling. Memories tumbled through her mind and led her back to when she stumbled and he had caught her. She was caught unawares by the rush of desire which deceived her into thinking she could smell his cologne again. Realising the time, she guiltily shot out of bed grabbing her dressing gown as she left the bedroom. There was no sign of George in the living room and Emma was sitting patiently waiting for her mother to get up, oblivious to the happenings of the night before.

"Hello, mam. Did you have a nice time at the dance?"

"Er... yes thanks, love. Have you seen your dad?"

"He went out. He said he was going up to Granny's house and that I wasn't to wake you."

Laura glanced at the clock on the mantelpiece and realised Emma would be hungry.

"Have you had any breakfast?"

"Dad did me some toast before he went out. I wanted to go with him to see Auntie Ev's baby, but he said I had to stay here."

"Well, give me a few minutes and then we'll go up there, shall we?"

Emma nodded her head and smiled excitedly. "Do you think Auntie Ev will let me hold the baby?"

"She might let you hold him on your knee if you sit down," Laura replied as she left to get dressed.

An hour later and they were almost there. Emma's legs had improved so much she no longer needed to be pushed in the chair. Her right leg was slightly thinner than the left but the only residual effect of the polio was a limp which only became noticeable when she was tired. At these times she would drag her right leg a little, but otherwise she had made a rapid and almost full recovery.

They walked into the house in Ramsden Avenue and found Mrs Taylor peeling potatoes for the family dinner. Laura was made welcome as usual and she was told that George was at the bottom of the garden with his father, helping to mow the lawn with an ancient contraption which passed as a lawn mower.

"Hello, Granny. Is Auntie Ev and Uncle Ray here? I want to see the baby."

"Uncle Ray's at work but Auntie Ev's through there," she pointed into the living room which looked as bright as a new pin.

Emma made a bee-line for the baby while Laura hung around hoping to ask if Mrs Taylor had noticed a difference in George. She was saved from having to ask outright when her mother-in-law looked sideways at her saying, "Our George is a bit miserable these days, Laura. What's got into him?"

"He doesn't sleep well, mam and he gets a lot of headaches. I'm a bit worried that his malaria might come back."

"It's always a possibility, I suppose. But there seems to be something else. Have you had a row?"

Laura sighed and tears flooded her eyes and threatened to overflow. She gulped her reply, "We have nothing but rows lately, mam. I can't do anything right." She took a deep breath, "He thinks there's something going on between me and Martin Beauchamp, but there isn't – I swear to it."

Laura reached for her handkerchief and Mrs Taylor patted her hand, "Don't worry, Laura. I'll have a word with him, if he'll listen that is."

"That's the problem, mam. He doesn't listen. He gets something fixed into his head and nothing will shift it."

"Pour him a cuppa and take it to him. Take one for dad, too. Are you staying for dinner?"

Laura drew a ragged breath to calm her emotions but her hands were shaking when she lifted the tea cups. "I'll ask him," she said with a wry smile.

George was surprised to see her and managed a half smile as he took the tea.

"Mam has asked us if we want to stay for dinner, George. What do you think?"

"Alright by me," he answered and turned away. Mr Taylor took his cup and thanked Laura.

"Where's that young granddaughter of mine? Did you bring her?" he asked

"'Course I did, dad. She's with your Ev, playing with the baby."

"She's a good lass, is our little Emma."

By the time the men had finished in the garden the dinner was on the table and it always amazed Laura how Mrs Taylor managed to feed so many with so little. There wasn't much meat on the plates but there were plenty of vegetables from the garden and everyone had the biggest Yorkshire pudding each. It had been baked in the side oven of the fire which Laura thought must make them taste even better.

When the washing up was done Laura hesitantly asked George if he wanted to go and look at the new house, which would be theirs in a few weeks. He surprised her by agreeing to go and Mrs Taylor winked at Laura as they left with Emma between them holding their hands. Laura wondered at the change in George and only hoped it would last. She thought of Martin and wondered how he was and if he was stiff and sore from George's punches.

"Which one is ours, mam?" Emma asked as they passed the new shops on the left.

"Just a bit further down past the lamppost," she answered.

They stopped at the gate of No. 31 Bowmandale and Laura looked at George, "Shall we go and have a look round the back?"

"Aye, go on then," he answered shortly.

Emma opened the gate and started to climb the three or four steps which took them up to an elevated level, down a passageway at the side of the house, and into the back garden. They looked through the kitchen window and Laura was pleased to see that there was a walk-in pantry and enough room for two armchairs by the fire. It all looked so bright and new, Laura couldn't help smiling and squeezing George's hand. He put his arm around her and pulled her towards him, kissing her cheek. She was amazed at this show of affection and grinned at him.

"Oh, George. We're going to be so happy here, aren't we?"

"I think we are, lass. I think we are."

Emma had gone up some more steps to the top of the garden. "Look mam, look dad. There's a really big garden here."

They followed her up the stone steps and saw the length of the garden was almost the size of an allotment on its own.

"This is going to keep me busy," George said.

"You'll get it sorted in no time, I know it."

"Come on, let's go and have a look in the front window." Emma was so excited she couldn't keep still.

They passed the washhouse, coalhouse and outside toilet as they followed her round the front. The bay window showed a nicely proportioned front room with a tiled fireplace.

"I can't wait to move in, George. Can you?" she smiled happily, so relieved that he was feeling so positive.

"Won't be long now, love," he said as they returned to street level.

FOURTEEN

Laura never did find out what had happened to change George's outlook, and in the end just accepted the fact that thankfully, he was amiable again. She visited Polly in the week and was relieved when Martin was absent and no one mentioned him.

It was a fortnight later and the longed for move had taken place when Chris drew up in the car to announce that Polly had gone into labour properly. Immediately she heard this she begged Chris to take her and Emma to The Elms so that she could help her sister if possible.

When she arrived she ran straight up the stairs to find Polly in a great deal of pain and discomfort. She remembered her own labour with Emma and sympathised, holding Polly's hand and talking to her when the pain became unbearable.

"Where's the doctor or the nurse?" Polly almost screamed.

"They're both busy with someone else at the moment, love," Laura replied.

"Where's Chris then?"

"He's with Emma downstairs. There's not much he can do anyway, is there? It's best that I stay with you for now."

As the pain faded once more, Polly gasped, "Was it like this for you, Laura?"

"It always is, Polly. It's just nature I'm afraid."

"To think this is what I've waited all these years for. I must've been mad." Another pain came and Polly gritted her teeth to suppress the desire to scream once more. It turned into a guttural moan just as the doorbell rang. They heard Chris answer the door and Nurse Beswick entered the room a couple of minutes later. She began to get things ready and automatically went to wash her hands, noting as she returned, that Polly was sweating and straining.

"Don't push yet, Polly. We don't want to hurt the baby."

"I can't help it. I feel as if I'm being split in two," she panted as Laura wiped her face with a cool flannel.

"How long have you had the pain?"

"Hours and hours. It started in the middle of the night but I didn't want to get you here and find it was a false alarm again."

"No fear of that – it's the real thing this time."

Nurse Beswick was a middle-aged woman and had been present at Emma's birth. She was a familiar figure riding her black bicycle around the town, her bag pushed forcefully into a wicker basket at the front of the bike. She had delivered more babies than she cared to remember in her long career, but had never had any of her own. She examined Polly and felt the contractions tighten her abdomen. They were strong and hard but the baby didn't seem to be making any headway. Not wanting to frighten her patient, she smiled and patted Polly's hand.

"Just a bit longer, Polly. Don't worry, your baby will be born when it's ready and not before."

She caught Laura's eye and managed to indicate with an imperceptible nod of her head that she wanted to speak to her.

"I'm just going to see if Mrs Garside can make us a cuppa, Polly. Do you want one?"

"Can I have some water, please?"

"I'll bring you some," she said hoping that she would take the hint and follow her to the kitchen.

"I'll come and help you," she replied, obviously having picked up on the ploy.

"Don't be long will you, Laura?"

"I'll be back in no time at all."

Down in the kitchen, Nurse Beswick aired her concerns about the baby and asked if she could use the telephone. She rang the doctor's surgery again and left a message with his wife that he should come directly to The Elms as soon as he returned. Chris was trying to amuse Emma but found he couldn't concentrate on anything. He was unaware of the nurse's concerns and was relieved when the doorbell rang again and the doctor walked in.

Laura and the nurse followed him up the stairs with the water Polly had asked for, and then she left them to it to go and speak with Chris. Mrs Garside took Emma into the kitchen and gave her some milk and biscuits so that the adults could speak freely without little ears flapping.

When Laura had relayed the nurse's concerns, Chris was ready to run up the stairs and see for himself what was going on, but Laura asked him to wait until the doctor had finished his examination. Ten minutes later his patience was rewarded when the doctor put his head round the door and said that the baby would be some time coming, but there were no problems as yet.

"Why is it taking so long, Doctor?" Chris asked, worry lines creasing his brow.

"Occasionally these things happen. It will just take its own time."

Impatient now with the non-answers to his questions Chris almost shouted, "Give me some indication as to

155

how long we can expect this to go on, Doctor, please." His exasperation was evident in his voice.

"I just don't know, Chris. Try not to worry and I'll keep you up to date with everything that happens."

Hour by hour they waited to hear news of the baby's arrival but nothing came. Polly's groans were audible downstairs now and Laura decided to take Emma home as it was time to get George some tea ready for when he came home from work. She promised she would be back as soon as possible and Chris was left alone to pace the floor.

As it was, Laura was unable to get back until quite late in the evening, and even then it was against George's wishes, but she was determined to be around for Polly if she needed her. George had been tired and unreasonable when he had returned from work and a row had ensued. Emma had been put to bed with promises of seeing the new baby when it arrived. George begrudgingly agreed to allow Laura to stay with Polly as long as Martin Beauchamp wasn't around. She managed to persuade him that she hadn't seen Martin since the night of the carnival dance and almost ran out of the house in her eagerness to get away.

The journey to The Elms was a great deal shorter than it had been and she ran up the ten-foot and into Park Avenue. She then cut through the park to arrive breathless about fifteen minutes later. She was dismayed to note that the doctor's car was still there and dreading the worst, she entered through the back door and into the kitchen where Chris, Mrs Garside, and to her delight, Martin, were sitting nursing cups of tea. Her heart skipped a beat as she looked at Martin before asking, "Is she alright?"

"Still no change, Laura," Chris answered, gripping his cup tightly.

"Come and join us, love. Pour yourself a cuppa," Mrs Garside suggested.

"I'll do it," Martin offered and indicated that she could take the chair next to his.

"I thought you'd gone away somewhere, Martin," she queried as she looked into his eyes. The damage George had done was almost healed and he bore only the slightest scar over his nose.

"I've been to see about re-enlisting. My old commanding officer says I can go back in at any time."

Laura was dumb struck and she took a gulp of tea to disguise her reaction. "That's a bit sudden isn't it?"

"I've been thinking about it for a couple of weeks now."

"Tell him not to go, Laura. We've only just got used to having him back," Mrs Garside interrupted.

Laura was about to reply when they heard an almighty scream emanating from upstairs and Chris was out of his seat in a flash.

"Polly!" he shouted and began to climb the stairs to the backstairs to the first floor. Everyone else stood around staring open-mouthed at each other and then they heard the sound of a baby's cry, muted at first and then louder.

"We have to go up," Laura decided and they all followed on her heels.

They were met by the sight of the nurse holding a tiny baby in a warm towel. The baby was smeared in blood and birthing fluid and she immediately thrust the tiny bundle into Laura's arms and asked her to wipe the baby clean.

"Is Polly alright?"

157

Nurse Beswick answered shortly, "Polly's had a fit I'm afraid and I'm needed in there. The doctor is seeing to her now."

"What does that mean?" Martin asked for all of them. Laura began to cry and he put his arm around her to comfort her.

Inside the bedroom Chris refused to leave his wife and paced up and down as the doctor and nurse did what they could to bring Polly round. The fit was leaving her and her body relaxed into unconsciousness, blood trickling from her mouth where she had bit her tongue. The nurse cleaned her up as best she could while the doctor left the room to go and wash his hands. He was met by three anxious faces all asking at once what was going on.

Laura was holding the baby, a little girl, cleaned up now and sleeping in a long cream nightdress, and wrapped in a white shawl embroidered with yellow ducks, her long black eyelashes fanning her creamy cheeks.

"Polly will be fine now," the doctor informed them. It was a difficult birth and I doubt if there will be another, but I must go and wash my hands and then I need to examine the baby. Laura, will you take her into the bedroom for me please?"

Laura was only too pleased to do so, and entered the bedroom where Chris was sitting next to the bed holding Polly's hand.

"Do you want to see your daughter, Chris?"

Chris looked dazed as Laura handed him the baby. He held his child awkwardly and then smiled as she opened her eyes and looked into his own. A feeling of warmth and love overwhelmed him as he held her gently and traced her smooth, soft cheek with his finger.

"Hello, my darling girl," he whispered as tears blurred his vision.

Laura watched the magic of parental love as it unfolded before her like the petals of a flower, and the lump in her own throat threatened to strangle her. A movement from the bed caught her attention and Polly opened her eyes and looked at Chris holding their baby.

"Can I see her?" she whispered as she moved her hand to touch the shawl. Her words were strangely slurred due to her swollen tongue.

Chris leaned over and kissed Polly's forehead and placed the now sleeping bundle in his wife's arms.

"She's the most beautiful baby I've ever seen, Polly. Thank you."

Laura decided to leave them alone for a few minutes and left the room. The doctor and nurse were standing just outside the door talking to the other interested parties and the conversation ceased as Laura closed the bedroom door. All were looking at her expectantly.

"Polly's fine and so is the baby," she said simply, "they're just having a few private minutes together. Will you wait a while Doctor before you examine the baby, she seems well enough? Let's go and have another cup of tea and then I'm sure they'll want to show their daughter off to you all."

They all, including the nurse and doctor, trouped down to the kitchen, relieved that it was all over.

***

It seemed like hours later when Laura arrived back home elated by the evening's events. She had refused

Martin's offer to drive her home and explained, regretfully, that George was under the impression that he was no longer in Barton. She entered through the back door and George was sitting in one of the fireside chairs dozing, a half empty cup sitting on the fire grate. She closed the door quietly and drew the curtains over the window behind the sink and draining board, trying not to wake him. Then, she went through the door into the hallway and up the stairs to see if Emma was asleep. The small bedroom that Emma occupied was at the front of the house and had a large 'jump-up' cupboard where she stored her books and a few of her clothes. The landing light had been left on for her but, Laura noted, Emma was now fast asleep.

She went into her own bedroom and closed the new, brightly coloured curtains which she had made herself especially for the new house, and turned on a bedside lamp. She was just about to get undressed when she heard George climbing the stairs.

"What time do you call this?" he asked grumpily.

Laura was tired and immediately upset that he hadn't even bothered to ask how Polly was.

"It took a long time, George. She had a very bad time but the baby's beautiful. Thanks for asking," she answered sarcastically.

"Huh," was the limit of his reply.

Laura took a deep breath. "I'm going down to make a cup of tea, do you want one?"

"No, I was only waiting up for you. Why didn't you wake me up?"

"You looked so peaceful I didn't want to spoil your sleep. I'll just make myself a drink and wash up and then I'll come up."

George climbed into bed and fell asleep almost immediately. He looked tired, and Laura felt her heart soften as she looked at him. She might not love him anymore but he was still her husband and the father of her child. If only things could be as they used to be. She switched off the bedside lamp and opened the curtains slightly to let in the light from a street lamp outside, then went downstairs. She washed the dishes George had used but decided not to have another drink herself. She was awash with tea and couldn't face another one, so she sat in front of the dying embers of a small fire which George had lit, and closed her eyes, thinking of the evening's events.

'Oh, Martin', she thought. 'Why did you have to come back again and stir up these feelings in me?'

How would she cope without him if he decided to re-enlist? She had somehow fallen in love without even noticing it had happened. The night of the carnival dance had just brought everything to a head. Her need for emotional, and physical love, was evident and she had no doubt that Martin would be only too pleased to supply both, but she was a married woman, and nothing could change that. She had seen so many marriages go wrong during the war when husbands were away fighting but she had remained true to George, and she always would, but she couldn't help her mind and body betraying him even when she tried to resist it.

At last she tired of her inward battles and joined George in their marital bed, very aware that they would remain as distant as two people could get.

FIFTEEN

Chris had only the weekend to enjoy his new daughter and care for Polly before going back to work. He would have liked to have applied for some holiday, but knew he would be expected back in the classroom. Babies were women's work as far as the headmaster was concerned, and he could leave Polly in the capable hands of Mrs Garside, and Laura, when she could get away. Martin had agreed to stay on for a couple of months just to give him peace of mind that there would be a man around if one was needed.

Polly on the other hand knew joy as she had never known it before. After great and lengthy deliberations, they had decided to name the baby Elizabeth after Chris's grandmother, but Polly immediately shortened it to Lizzie. Her initial discomfort after giving birth vanished quickly and her energy soon returned. She was determined to look after Lizzie herself and refused point blank any suggestion of a nanny to help her.

"I've waited so long for this to happen, I'm not going to hand over my baby to anyone else," was her final word on the subject and Chris knew better than to press the point.

Looking after Lizzie became all-consuming and Polly spent hours just watching her sleep. Her first smile, her first tooth and her first taste of solid food was captured on camera and placed into an album for posterity. She didn't even notice when Chris began to spend his lunch times at work and stay later in the evening to catch up on his marking, such was her devotion to her daughter.

***

Mrs Garside watched and wondered at how Polly could so quickly neglect her husband and shook her head in exasperation at her selfishness. She would have spoken to Laura about it but she had her own problems with a recurrence of George's malaria during the late summer months and her visits were less frequent now.

***

Martin had moved away as he had said he would. The house was empty without him, with Chris spending so much time at work and Polly oblivious to everything except her precious daughter. Mrs Garside wondered what she should do, but realised that all she could do was keep her nose out of it and carry on caring for them as she always had done and hope that Polly would come to her senses before it was too late. If only Laura would visit again, perhaps she could say something.

As if her thoughts had carried themselves through the streets, there was a knock on the back door and Laura walked in as large as life.

"Hello, Mrs Garside. Is Polly in or has she taken Lizzie out for a stroll?"

"Laura!" Mrs Garside was amazed to see her so soon after thinking about her.

"Are you alright? You look as if you've seen a ghost. It's been a while since I was here, hasn't it?"

Mrs Garside smiled. "It's just that I was thinking about you and here you are. Polly's upstairs in the living room with Lizzie. She said it's too damp to take her out today."

"It's not that bad. The mist's lifted and the sun's come out."

"She'll be pleased to see you, Laura. Go up if you want to, but I'd like a quiet word with you....."

Just then Polly came into the kitchen with an empty feeding bottle.

"Laura, look. Lizzie's finished her bottle again. She's getting really big now."

"Hello, Polly. How are you?"

"Me? On top of the world of course, why wouldn't I be? Come and see Lizzie, she's smiling such a lot now and has two teeth at the bottom and the other's are coming through at the top."

Laura began following Polly out of the kitchen but turned and rolled her eyes at Mrs Garside in understanding.

Lizzie was indeed a beguiling little thing at five months old, and Laura understood her sister's passion for her, but she was the sole topic of conversation. There were no reciprocating questions as to how George, or Emma were getting on, or indeed how Laura was herself.

"I'm going to get some new blankets for her cot as soon as I can get to the shops. The weather's not been too good, has it? Do you remember last year and what it was like then?" Polly drew a breath and Laura intervened before she could start again.

"I don't think anyone will forget last Christmas in a hurry. How are you and Chris? Is he alright?"

"I think so. He's decided to stay at work just lately instead of coming home for his dinner. He knows how busy I am with Lizzie, and doesn't like to interrupt me."

"Oh, I see. Can I make a cup of tea, Polly? Do you want one?"

"Yes please. Ask Mrs Garside for some of those scones she made yesterday. Oh, look, Laura – Lizzie's smiling."

Laura went out into the hallway shaking her head. Mrs Garside was boiling the kettle ready to make their tea when she arrived in the kitchen.

"You've read my mind, Mrs Garside. Polly says have you got some of the scones you made yesterday?"

"I'll put some on a plate for you, Laura. I wanted to have a word with you - do you have a few minutes?"

"I don't think she'll notice I've even left the room," Laura answered raising her eyebrows expressively.

"I'm worried about her, Laura. Every new mother dotes on their baby but Polly's taking it to extremes. She even sleeps in the nursery now so that she can keep an eye on her during the night."

"That doesn't sound right." Laura chewed her thumb nail distractedly.

"I know. Chris spends nearly all his time at work since Christmas. How's George by the way? Is he feeling any better?"

"He's still weak and bad tempered. I don't know what to do for him anymore. I can't talk to Polly about it as she's only interested in Lizzie, so it gets a bit lonely not having someone to talk to."

"You can always come here, you know that."

"It's difficult getting away. I'm only here now because I was going to the market to get some shopping."

"Sounds like you don't need any more worries then, but I wondered if you could have a word with Polly about the way she treats Chris. He's not even allowed to hold Lizzie now in case he drops her. I ask you – is that anyway to treat the father of your child?"

166

"I'll see what I can do. I'd better take this tray up and try and talk some sense into her."

Polly had just finished changing a nappy when Laura entered the room, tray in hand.

"Put her down for a sleep, Polly. We haven't had a natter for ages for one reason or another. Come and have a scone and cup of tea."

"She likes to go to sleep in my arms, Laura. I'll be there in a minute."

Polly hoisted Lizzie into her arms and was about to go out of the room to dispose of the nappy.

"Let me hold her, Polly. I'll look after her until you get back."

"Oh, I don't usually leave her with anybody else. I won't be a minute."

"I'm not just anybody else, I'm her aunt."

"Well, you know what I mean," Polly smiled and left the room.

Laura sighed in exasperation and poured the tea. She wriggled back into the comfortable chair and nibbled her scone. How on earth was she supposed to broach the subject of Polly's marriage and her over-protectiveness of Lizzie? She looked around the room and wondered if Polly ever thought how lucky she was to have such a house to live in. Thinking of her own sparsely furnished home she couldn't help but feel a little envious and was determined to knock some sense into her younger sister's head.

She noticed a pile of newspapers by the fireside and guessed they were there ready to light the fires in the morning. She knew that Polly employed a part-time cleaner and presumed that she had lit the fires earlier in the day and then gone home. She bent down to retrieve one of Lizzie's toys which had fallen down by the

167

papers and noticed an envelope sticking out from under the chair. Gingerly, she pulled it out and was surprised to find it had her name on it. She was still looking at the envelope when Polly returned.

"What's this, Polly? It's got my name on it."

"Oh, that. Yes, I'm sorry, I forgot to mention it. Martin left it for you when he went away."

"But that was months ago!" Laura was incredulous.

"I know, but like I said, I forgot." Polly began settling herself and Lizzie on the sofa and jumped as Laura slammed the envelope down hard on the table."

"What's the matter?" Polly sounded surprised.

"What's the matter?" Laura's breath was short with temper as she leaned forward, her eyes blazing. "This letter has been left here for you to give to me and you've just left it for months on end without even mentioning it. What's got into you, Polly?"

Polly shrugged, and started cuddling Lizzie who had started to mewl after Laura's outburst. "I didn't think it was that important."

"It might not be important to you, but it is to *me*!"

"Well you've got it now, haven't you?"

Laura stood up and started pacing the floor, trying to hold herself in check. What she really wanted to do was slap Polly's face for being so selfish but she knew she couldn't do that, so she counted to twenty before speaking.

"I think you should realise a few things, Polly. It might hurt to hear them, but you're going to hear them anyway."

Polly said nothing and looked into her sleeping child's face, ignoring her sister altogether.

Sitting down again in her chair Laura began, "Do you ever go out with Chris, Polly?"

"Of course we do, we take Lizzie out for a walk at the weekends. I push her in her pram and sometimes Chris comes with me."

"No, I mean – just you two, without Lizzie."

"No. I can't leave my precious girl. Anyway, Chris is usually busy doing his lesson plans for his classes, or marking their books."

Laura wanted to broach the subject of their sleeping arrangements but didn't know how to go about it. Then she had an inspiration.

"I'll bring Emma over one day and you and Chris can go out together. We'll stay with Lizzie until you come back. You could go across to Hull on the ferry and do some shopping."

"I've just told you, I never leave her. Never!"

"Well, you have to leave her at night, don't you? She sleeps in the nursery."

"I sleep in there with her. It's easier than disturbing Chris every time she cries for her bottle."

"She must be going through the night now. She's five months old."

"Chris sleeps better without me."

"Has he told you that?"

"No, but he never complains so he must do."

"I don't know what to say to you, Polly. You have a saint for a husband. Doesn't he ask you to sleep with him sometimes?"

"He used to, but I think he's got used to it now. He knows I have to stay with Lizzie."

"I think you're being very selfish."

Polly looked shocked, "And I think you're being very nosey asking me all these private questions. I don't ask you about George, do I?"

"No, Polly, you don't. But that's because you're so wrapped up in Lizzie. You've changed completely since she was born. I don't know you anymore."

"Well, you know where the door is, Laura. I suggest you go through it and leave me and my baby alone."

"You're going to regret this. There's trouble coming your way if you don't buck your ideas up."

Laura grabbed the unopened envelope stuffing it in her pocket as she left the room, closing the door quietly behind her. Back in the kitchen she told Mrs Garside some of what had happened but not all, leaving the older woman wringing her hands with worry.

***

Chris was alone in the classroom after all the children had gone home. It was dark outside and snow was falling. He finished his marking and was writing out the next day's arithmetic on the blackboard before finishing for the day. Mr Ross had already been in to check when he would be going home and had left a key for him to lock up. All he had to do was drop it off at the school house next door before going home.

He put the chalk down and stood back to look at the work he had set for his class, but his heart wasn't really in it. He walked to the window and looked out at the snow which had settled since darkness had fallen and sighed, running his hands through his hair in indecision. He knew he didn't want to go home. What did he have there except a wife who couldn't care less whether he was home or not? The thought pierced his heart like an arrow and his eyes filled with unshed tears. He remembered how he had prayed for a child for Polly a couple of Christmases back. A knock on the window separating the classroom from the hallway brought him out of his reverie. Miss Jenny Carlisle, the new infant teacher, waved to him and, blinking rapidly to disperse the threatened tears, he went to the door.

"You're working late too, are you?" she asked.

"I've just finished. It's a good job you knocked on the window. I didn't know anyone else was still here. I might have locked you in for the night."

She laughed, "You're right. I don't think I'd like to stay here too long into the night. It's a bit creepy when you're alone, isn't it?"

"I don't really think about it, but I suppose you could be right."

"I'll say goodnight then." She moved away to pick up some exercise books which she had left on a shelf next to the school bell. They were a bit unwieldy so Chris went to help. "Thanks very much. I'll see you tomorrow then," she smiled. Her lips parted over white, even teeth and Chris was mesmerised for a second. He looked into her eyes and noticed they were the purest green.

Realising he had been looking at her for a lot longer than he ought, he moved away, his face reddening slightly with embarrassment. He moved to open the door for her and inadvertently brushed her hand. The electricity passing between them was tangible and he withdrew his hand as if he'd been burned, causing her to drop the books.

"Oh dear! We don't seem to be having much luck, do we?" she laughed to cover any awkwardness.

"Let's start again then." Chris bent down with her to gather the books and caught the scent of her wavy, blonde hair, sending his senses reeling once more. His hands were trembling as he fumbled with the books but finally managed to gather them up again and piled them into her arms.

"Thanks again. See you tomorrow."

"Yes. See you tomorrow."

Chris went back into the classroom and sat at his desk trying to recover his composure. The emotions he had felt just then were almost alien to him now. It had been a long time since he had been attracted to anyone, including his wife, in such a way. He thought of Polly at home with Lizzie. She wouldn't be waiting for him, of course, she never was. He didn't think she would notice if he didn't go home at all. He started to put his coat on and turned out the light to the classroom, and then remembered the key to lock up was on his desk.

It was cold outside and, once he had returned the key to the school house, he had to walk briskly to keep warm. He was hurrying along Priestgate when he noticed Miss Carlisle struggling to open her front door. It was a narrow one-windowed frontage with a dark blue door and the street-lighting was very poor. He approached her and took the books out of her arms so that she could insert the key properly.

"Yet again you come to my rescue."

"Knight in shining armour, that's me," he replied jokingly.

The front door stood ajar and she stepped over the threshold into the narrow hallway and switched on a lamp. The living room overlooked the street and the lamp cast a cosy glow through the window. Chris was still at the door with the books so she took them from him and stood aside invitingly.

"Would you like a cup of tea or something before you leave?"

Chris was sorely tempted to accept her offer but thought better of it. He was afraid of the intensity of his own feelings, thinking how easy it would be to step into that room. It looked so invitingly cosy and intimate but he knew instinctively that if he did, then his integrity would be lost forever.

"Thank you, but no. My housekeeper will have a meal ready for me."

"Maybe another time then," she said and closed the door.

Chris walked away wondering if he had done the right thing and when he opened the front door at The Elms, he heard Polly singing to Lizzie in the way she always did when she bathed her, so he took off his coat and shoes and ventured upstairs.

"Hello, Polly. Hello, my little sweetheart," he said as he opened the bathroom door.

"Don't open the door too wide, Chris. You'll let a draught in and Lizzie will catch cold." Polly's voice was less than welcoming.

There it was again, the feeling that he was surplus to requirements in his own house. He pressed a kiss on Lizzie's chubby, red cheeks, and tried to kiss Polly but she moved to reach for a towel and he was rebuffed once more. He slid out of the bathroom as quickly as possible and went to eat his tea in the kitchen. At least Mrs Garside always seemed to enjoy his company, but he thought of the inviting living room he had seen earlier and pondered on what delightful company Jenny Carlisle might prove to be.

That night he stretched out in his lonely bed and remembered the scent of her hair and the softness of the waves which fell around her face. Those greener than green eyes which held so much invitation and the

173

peaches and cream complexion he wanted so much to touch.

SIXTEEN

Earlier that day Laura had walked out of The Elms with the intention of never going back, but by the time she reached the Market Place and bought what she needed for the evening meal, she had calmed down enough to start worrying about Polly instead.

The day was cold and it had already rained but small flakes of snow began to fall as she ventured into the Singing Kettle café for a cup of tea. A steamy interior and the clatter of cups and saucers welcomed her as she found a seat at an empty table. She put her basket on the chair next to the wall and went to the counter. She recognised the woman serving as Millie Cartwright and was surprised to see her.

"Hello, Millie. I thought you'd gone off to America when you married that GI?"

Millie raised her eyes heavenward, "I did, but I soon regretted it, Laura. If you think Barton's a bit backward then think again. His home town was in the middle of nowhere and I was treated like a slave. His family expected me to wait on them hand and foot and as soon as I could get the money together, I came home. Mam managed to scrape up enough to send me half of the air fare. We're getting divorced. I know it's looked down on, but I was really miserable and I almost kissed the ground when I got back. I'm never leaving again, never."

"I'm sorry to hear that, Millie. I didn't know your husband to talk to but he seemed a nice quiet bloke."

"He was till we got back to America. Do you know, Laura, they treat the black people there really badly. I felt so sorry for them. They're really looked down on because of their colour. We were in the south where they used to use them as slaves, and I'm telling you, they're not treated much better now. I'm glad to be out of it."

Laura picked up her cup and saucer, "Good luck to you now then, Millie. I hope you find someone else."

"I'm not bothered if I don't. My mam says men are all the same, so I'm gonna enjoy life a bit now I'm back."

Smiling to herself, Laura went back to her table with her cup of tea, trying not to slop it into the saucer. She remembered Millie from her school days and when war broke out the Yanks came over in their hundreds. She was one of many to be found doing their courting in the long grass on the Humber bank.

Taking a deep breath she rummaged in her coat pocket to find the envelope which Martin had left for her. She had been impatient to read it since finding it, and this was the first opportunity she had had. She prayed fervently that no one would come and sit at the same table and deprive her of the pleasure.

My Darling Laura

I hope you don't mind me addressing you this way, but to me you are just that. I know I have no right to love you, but please believe me that I do, with all my heart.

I hope also that you will forgive me for leaving you. It's not what I want, but what I want - I know I can't have. You are out of my reach, Laura, so I must put myself out of yours. I can't stand by and want you so badly and know that you belong to George. It breaks my heart to leave you but I know it's for the best. If I stayed it would make us both miserable because I know you feel the same way about me. You have never said so because you aren't free to declare it, but I know nonetheless.

I've decided not to re-enlist, although my family think I have, so please don't say anything to them. There's an opening in the Diplomatic Service in Hong Kong which I've an option to take up, but first I'm going to see a bit of the world in peace time rather than war, then I'll decide what to do with my life. I'll get in touch with Chris eventually with an address, but until then you won't know where I am.

So, my dearest girl, I'll say goodbye for now, and wish you every happiness in the future, - I only wish I could be there to share it with you. I'll think of you every day.

Your loving friend
Martin x x x

Laura took a deep, ragged breath and reached in her coat pocket for a handkerchief. It had been three months since he had left and this letter had been waiting for her since then. She couldn't believe how Polly was so dismissive of her own forgetfulness and she felt her temper start to rise again, so she put the letter away at the bottom of her shopping bag. She would have to dispose of it at some point, even though she wanted to keep it and read it again and again, but she would have to wait until George was out of the house and then she would read it just once more and then burn it.

She looked at the clock on the opposite wall and knew she would have to go and pick Emma up from school. The snow had turned to sleet and she turned her collar up on her coat before stepping out into the cold afternoon. Emma was waiting with her coat on when she arrived at the Church School. She was sitting in the entrance porch where the coat pegs had held children's coats for more than a hundred years.

"You're late, mam. What's the matter, have you been crying?"

Laura hadn't realised she looked upset and answered lightly, "No, silly. The wind's getting up and it's made my eyes run."

"My leg's been hurting a bit today but I'll try to hurry."

"Come on then, but don't hurt yourself. We'll get home soon enough."

***

It was summer time and although George was feeling unwell again, he knew he would have to carry on regardless and go to work. His train to New Holland would be leaving soon so he would have to get a move on or he would miss the connection with the ferry which would take him across the Humber to Hull. The day looked promising with blue skies and the chatter of early morning birds as he hurried down to the station carrying his donkey jacket and sandwich tin. This was the only drawback with moving house, he thought, it was a lot further away from the station and consequently he was always tired when he arrived. Thankfully, as he got there his pal, Doggie Barker, was waiting for him and helped him aboard just as the whistle blew.

"Thought you weren't gonna make it, George. You're later than ever today. What's up?"

"I'll be alright, just a bit breathless. Nice day though."

"Take it easy for a bit then and don't rush once we get there. Work'll be there when we aren't," Doggie was unusually philosophical today.

The train had a corridor which ran the length of the carriage leading into small compartments, seating six or so people and he and Doggie found seats together. George stared at the glass-framed photographs of various scenes which hung over the opposite seats and wondered what those places were like. Some of them had names underneath but the print was too small to read at any great distance. He recognised a picture of Lincoln Cathedral and presumed that the others were scenes from rural Lincolnshire.

"You look a bit peaky today, George. Are you sure you're up to a day's work."

"I don't seem to be able to get my breath very well."

The engineering works where George and Doggie worked as welders was contracted to help repair a large ship which meant they often had to work in dangerous conditions, either deep in the bowels or higher up between decks, and the safety ropes and scaffolding sometimes hampered them in their job.

The ferry ride over the water seemed to revive him a little and he was able to walk the distance to the shipyard without any problems. His heart sank when he discovered the gaffer for that particular shift was none other than Stan Greenwood, well-known bully and company man. He also cut corners if he thought it would get the job done quicker and cheaper, and had been known to sack someone on the spot if he thought they were slacking. George knew better than to ask for any favours from him. Stan was ticking names off a sheet of paper held to a board with a bulldog clip and looked at his watch as the two men approached.

"A minute later and you'd be on your way 'ome," he said sourly.

"I'll bring a set of oars next time, Mr Greenwood."

"Don't come it with me, Barker or you'll need damned oars to get back ower river."

Doggie looked sheepish and George gazed at the floor trying not to smile. He had met men like Stan Greenwood when he was in the army. They sucked up to the officers but would run a mile if a favour was needed by a mate. Not that Stan Greenwood had many mates, even the bosses didn't like him much but he got the work done and that's all they were bothered about.

He had an impossibly boyish face with puffy tight skin and rosy cheeks and he was the only gaffer George knew who wore a bowler hat to work, covering his curly, ginger hair. His blue overalls were spotlessly clean and his white shirt singled him out as the man in charge and many felt sorry for his poor, brow-beaten wife who had to wash and iron his work clothes at the end of every shift. "You're up there, Taylor." He pointed to the ribs of the ship which were exposed for repair and welding. George's expression must have betrayed his thoughts, as Stan added, "And you can take that look off yer face, there's plenty of men out there would jump at the chance of working 'ere. You, Barker, you're on t'other side."

When neither man moved, he added, "Go on then, get a move on or you'll be getting your cards. I can't abide slackers," he mumbled as he walked away.

Doggie was about to put in his five penn'orth when George grabbed him and led him towards their working area.

"Come on, we both need the money. If we keep our noses down maybe he'll leave us alone."

"Not much chance of that, is there?"

"Not much, no, but we can try."

Welding was hot work at any time, but as the sun rose higher in the sky, George stopped for a moment to wipe his face on his shirt sleeve. He glanced over to where Doggie was working a few stages down on the opposite side of the ship and realised that it would be even hotter during the afternoon as the sun moved round.

There was a movement at his arm and he looked up to see an apprentice had approached him. He recognised him as Billy Turner, a nice young lad of about eighteen, who lived with his widowed mother in Hull. He was fresh-faced with bright, wide eyes and an innocent expression.

"Mr Taylor?" Billy turned his cap around in his hands in a nervous fashion.

"Hello, Billy. What can I do for you?"

"I don't want to cause any trouble like, but I've been told to work alongside you and I'm a bit worried about the ropes on yon scaffold. They look a bit frayed to me."

"Have you asked Mr Greenwood about it?"

"I daren't mention it to him. You know what he's like."

"Aye, I do, but you could ask the union rep to mention it if you don't want to do it yourself."

"Who is it on this shift, Mr Taylor?"

"Try Len Burkett. He's a good bloke, but don't do 'owt till dinner time or you'll be in trouble with old Greenwood."

Billy smiled at George and began to ready himself for work.

"What do you want me to do, Mr Taylor?"

Billy was in the second year of his apprenticeship and held promise to be a good welder. George took him through a few stages of what he was doing and then told him to move to another joint and try repeating the process. By lunch time, the sun was high in the sky and the works hooter sounded to announce it was time to down tools and take a break.

"Come on, lad," George moved over to Billy. "Let's go and have a look at them ropes you were telling me about."

They moved further along the scaffolding and Billy pointed to a place where nuts and bolts had come out of the scaffold and had been hastily replaced by old rope.

"I see what you mean, Billy. Let's go and see if we can find Len."

They took their sandwich boxes down to ground level and went to the canteen where it was a lot cooler, and sitting at one of the tables drank their tea and ate their sandwiches, whilst waiting to see if Len Burkett came in. It wasn't until their break was almost over and they were returning to work when they spotted him with Stan Greenwood. They appeared to be having a heated discussion and Len was pointing up at the scaffolding. Stan jabbed his finger into Len's chest repeatedly, and made some remark which was out of earshot to George and Billy. Len retaliated by pushing Stan against the toilet block wall but he recovered himself and puffed out his chest shouting, "You'll regret that, Len Burkett, just see if you don't."

He pushed his way past the union man and headed towards the offices where he would no doubt report the incident.

George and Billy went up to Len, "What's up Len? What's he done now?"

"I've just been pointing out some safety issues, George, but *Mr Greenwood* doesn't think they're relevant."

"We were gonna point out the ropes on the scaffold. Young Billy here spotted them this morning."

"That's one of the things I was raising with him. I shouldn't have lost my temper but I hate people poking me in the chest, especially idiots like him."

"We'd better get back, Billy," George said. "You watch out for Greenwood now, Len. He'll be after you."

"Don't I know it?"

As the afternoon wore on, George and Billy moved along the wooden platform. The goggles they were supposed to wear to protect their eyes made them sweat even more and many men refused to wear them and consequently suffered from red-eye when sparks flew into their eyes. Billy took off his goggles and wiped his face once more, looking up at the sun's position. He glanced over to where George was working and decided to have a breather while he watched the older man tackle a tricky weld. Unfortunately, he forgot to put his goggles back on and approached George from behind. George moved position slightly to look beneath the place he was welding leaving the torch he was using aimed at the steel. Billy consequently walked into a face full of sparks which made him jump back instinctively. The next thing he knew he had stepped backwards off the scaffold with one foot and his cries and flailing arms caught George unawares.

Billy managed to grab a rope which dangled from one of the poles and George was teetering on the brink of the platform. He managed to stop himself falling by clinging to the equipment he had been using but with his weight it began inching itself towards the edge. He steadied himself quickly and looked down to see Billy dangling in mid-air on the end of the rope. Billy's shouts had been heard by other men who came running along the scaffolding to help.

George lay on his stomach and began hauling on the rope. Billy was no lightweight and was too terrified to do anything to help. By the time the others had reached them, he was lying prone on the platform gasping for breath. George, on the other hand, was lying on his back clutching at his chest. He heard someone shout for a first aid team and dimly saw Billy kneeling beside him.

"Mr Taylor. Are you alright?" He sounded close to tears but George couldn't breathe let alone speak and the pains in his chest were becoming unbearable. His last thoughts were of Laura and Emma, before a stretcher crew arrived and he lost consciousness. Billy insisted on going to the hospital with him and Len Burkett accompanied them too. The ambulance crew did everything they could to make him comfortable, but George's heart gave up the struggle for life before reaching their destination.

SEVENTEEN

Laura was sitting in her kitchen two weeks after George's funeral. The fine weather had given way to rain and a drop in temperature but she didn't care one way or the other. People had been very kind and even Polly, once she had heard the news of George's fatal accident, had visited without Lizzie in tow. She had been kind and almost like her old self but was constantly watching the clock in case she was late back. In the end, Laura had almost lost her temper and told her to go, but decided that it really didn't matter. The visitors had tailed off now and were getting on with their own lives, and Laura understood without anyone having to tell her, that she must get on with her own. The trouble was she didn't have the first clue about what to do but the rent still had to be paid.

There was a knock on the back door and opening it she found Billy Turner standing there, cap in hand.

"Hello, Mrs Taylor. I just wondered if it was alright to come and see you for a few minutes."

"Of course you can, Billy. Have you come all the way over from Hull just to see me?"

"I've taken a day's holiday so don't worry that I'll be losing any wages. I just wanted to come and see how you were."

Laura choked back her urge to cry when she looked at him. He felt guilty about George's death, she could tell, and needed to have some kind of absolution from her.

"Come in, Billy. I'll make us a cup of tea. I've made some cakes for Emma's tea but she won't eat all these, so we'll have some shall we?"

Billy looked at the two fireside chairs and the look on his face told Laura that he knew that one had been George's. Laura caught the look and said, "You sit in my chair and I'll sit here."

Billy threw her a look of gratitude and sat down in front of the meagre fire which took the chill off the air. Laura lit the gas under the kettle and set the table with three cups and saucers. "Emma will be home soon. She says she's too old now to be taken and fetched from school so I've had to let her do it. She comes home with a couple of girls from across the road."

When the tea was made and the cakes had been placed in the centre of the red chenille cloth, Billy moved from the fire and joined Laura at the table.

"I still feel so guilty about George, Mrs Taylor. I can't sleep for thinking about him and it all goes over and over in my head."

"You mustn't feel guilty, Billy. George had a bad heart and it was a miracle he managed for as long as he did. You heard what the doctor at the inquest said. The malaria and dysentery he suffered in the war was too much for him."

"I know, but if I'd only stayed put instead of being nosey, George would still be here." His eyes welled with tears and he looked away uncomfortably. Laura put her hand over his to comfort him.

"Don't torture yourself with this, lad. I've gone over it in my mind too, and as I see it, George went the way he would have wanted, helping you to live."

Billy broke down completely at her words, and she patted his hand and gave him a handkerchief. "Come on, love. Have a drink of tea - it'll make you feel better."

He took a ragged breath and wiped his eyes and blew his nose. "Thanks, Mrs Taylor. You're very brave."

"Life tends to make you hard when you've suffered as many knocks as I have. It doesn't necessarily make you brave it just makes things easier to deal with."

"Mrs Taylor?" Billy began again but Laura interrupted him,

"Call me Laura. Mrs Taylor is my mother-in-law," she smiled.

"Oh alright, Laura, then, I've come on behalf of George's work mates as well as myself." He stood up and removed an envelope from his jacket pocket. "We had a collection like, and they said I could bring it. I hope you don't mind."

Laura looked startled and was hesitant in taking the proffered envelope. "What is it, Billy?"

"It's fifty pounds. We collected it in the canteen and everybody wanted to put something in. He was a nice bloke, George, and well liked."

Laura stared at the money in the envelope but didn't know what to say. This was so unexpected. She could no longer hold the tears back and she put her head in her hands and wept. Billy didn't know what to do so he sat down again and the roles were reversed as he patted her hand and poured her another cup of tea.

"I'm really sorry I've made you cry, Laura," he ventured at last once her sobbing had calmed down.

Laura raised her head and managed a crooked smile. "Don't worry, lad. I needed to cry and that was the first time since I heard about George's accident. I was beginning to think I wasn't normal."

187

He didn't really understand what she was saying, but at least she had stopped crying.

They finished their tea and Billy washed up the cups and saucers before he left. He turned to her as he set foot outside the back door, "You will be alright, Laura, won't you?"

"Don't you worry, Billy, I'll be fine and please thank all the people who put into the collection for me, won't you?"

"I will. Bye then."

"Bye, Billy. Thanks again for coming all this way. You won't need to lose any more sleep now, will you?"

"No, I feel better too, Laura. Thanks again."

Emma came home just as Billy was going out through the gate at the bottom of the steps. She didn't speak to him but he looked at her and nodded as he closed the gate. She ran into the house asking who the boy was and Laura showed her the money that had been collected on George's behalf.

"Will we be able to stay here then, mam? We won't have to move again, will we?"

"No, we can stay here until I can get a job at least. This will pay the rent and buy us food for a long time if we're careful."

Emma clapped her hands and reached for a cake off the plate which Laura had left for her. She was constantly amazed at how resilient Emma had been at the news of George's death. Of course, there had been heartbreak and questions but she had recovered reasonably quickly. The funeral had been traumatic for her, but since then she had adjusted very well. In fact, she had been Laura's rock, someone to get up for, and look after, someone who needed her.

"Will you have to go out to work, mam?"

"I suppose I'll have to or we won't be able pay the rent. Maybe I can get a part time job at Hoppers again or maybe in a shop. The only problem will be your holiday times and weekends.

"I could stay with Aunty Polly, couldn't I?"

"I don't know about that, love. Polly's been a bit wrapped up in herself since Lizzie was born and we haven't seen much of her."

Emma nodded silently. Laura had noticed how she had been quite hurt by Polly's attitude since Lizzie came into the world, but she hoped her sister would come to her senses soon.

***

A month later, Laura still hadn't found any kind of work which took into account Emma's school hours and she was beginning to worry that she would never find anything. Polly had visited only once during that month and hadn't offered to look after Emma during the holidays.

Emma was in bed one night when someone knocked on the back door. Laura opened the door and was amazed to find Mr Roberts from the Prudential standing on the doorstep as they hadn't been able to afford to give him any money for months.

"Hello, Laura. Can I come in?"

"You can, but I don't have anything to give you I'm afraid. As you know things are really tight at the moment."

"I know. That's what I'm here for."

Intrigued, she stood back to let him in and went to stand by the table. He had a black satchel over his shoulder which usually held the pennies and shillings people handed over once a week to save for a rainy day. He undid the clasp at the front and pulled out a book, laying it in front of her on the table.

"What's this?" she asked, puzzled.

"It's the payments George made into a life insurance policy since he started work. He always made sure he paid something in every pay day before he brought his wages home to you. He didn't want you to know about it until after his death. He used to call at the offices on his way to the ferry every pay day without fail. We've taken a long time to get everything together as we had to transfer money from the account in Hull to yours in Barton. I'm sorry it's taken so long but you wouldn't believe the red tape we have to deal with along with forms for everything under the sun."

Laura lifted the book and opened it up, noting the payments of two shillings per week for months. At the end of the columns of figures was stamped CLOSED in black print.

"What happens to the money now, Mr Roberts?"

"We pay you now, Laura. You can have it monthly or weekly but it's a tidy sum he was insured for. Here's the policy for you to look at."

Laura took the large folded paper and opened it next to the book. She didn't understand the wording at all and looked at Mr Roberts for help.

"George was insured for £5,000, Laura, and we now pay you instead of the other way round. As I said, you can decide on how you want it. If you want the whole amount at once then we can do that as well, but usually people have it weekly."

"I'm a bit overwhelmed, Mr Roberts. I'd no idea George had done anything like this."

"I know. He was most insistent that you shouldn't be told until you needed it, so to speak." He shifted uncomfortably.

Laura sat down heavily in her chair, her face ashen and her fingers trembling. Her thoughts reeled at the prospect of having so much money and couldn't believe George had done this without her knowing.

"I'm sorry it's come as a shock, but we had to abide by his wishes."

"Yes, I know. But can you leave this with me and I'll let you know when I've had a chance to think about it?"

"Tell you what. I'll pop back on Thursday night and you can let me know then. Is that alright?"

"Yes, I should know by then. Thanks, Mr Roberts."

She rose to show him to the door and leaned against it when he had gone. This was a real turn up for the books. She couldn't believe George had kept something like this from her, but acknowledging that they hadn't really had much of a marriage for the last couple of years she took her seat once more in front of the fire and thought about hers and Emma's future.

***

Polly was at home as usual, busying herself with washing a few of Lizzie's clothes. Lizzie was upstairs in the nursery sleeping the sleep of the innocent and Mrs Garside was sitting in the kitchen watching Polly with a steady gaze. Chris was out at one of his meetings.

"What are you staring at, Mrs Garside?" Polly asked. She could feel the woman's eyes on her, boring into her back just between the shoulder blades.

"If you want an honest answer, Polly, I'm staring at the silliest young woman I've ever met."

Polly turned around aghast at the older woman's words.

"What do you mean?"

"I'll tell you what I mean. I've kept it inside me for the past nine months, since that little baby made an appearance, but I can't keep it in any more."

"Kept what in?"

"My feelings, that's what."

"Yes, but your feelings about what?" Polly felt like she was drawing teeth.

Mrs Garside took a deep breath, knowing that this would either make or break her friendship and perhaps even get her the sack. "Ever since Lizzie was born you've changed from a lovely, gentle, caring, young woman into a mad, obsessed mother who doesn't give a thought to her husband, her sister or anyone else come to that."

Awareness suddenly dawned in Polly's eyes but she still tried to shrug off the blame. "I can't be the same person I was, Mrs Garside. I've got responsibilities now. Lizzie needs me."

"Yes, and so had Laura got responsibilities when you came home, but she was there for you, wasn't she? Now the poor woman has had to deal with Emma's illness and now her husband's death and you've maybe been to see her twice since he died. You should be ashamed of yourself."

"I'll go tomorrow. Will that suit you?"

"No, Polly, it won't. You're going to have to do a lot of thinking about yourself and your marriage, as well as your sister and niece, or you're going to end up without any of them."

"Chris is busy with his school work. You know that. If I didn't find things to do here I'd go mad waiting for him all the time." She was feeling petulant and annoyed at the accusations being thrown at her.

"That poor man must feel like a stranger in his own home. You're always too busy to sit with him, eat with him, or generally talk to him, when he comes home. I wouldn't blame him if he found someone else and that's putting it straight."

"Chris wouldn't do that," Polly said incredulously.

"He's a man isn't he?" On those words Mrs Garside grabbed her knitting off the table and stomped up the stairs. She stopped half way up and turned, "I'm having an early night. I'll see you in the morning, but you think on, young lady. A lot of people think the world of you for some reason, and it's about time you came to your senses."

Polly dropped the cardigan she had been rinsing out back into the water and went to sit at the chair Mrs Garside had just vacated. She had never been spoken to like that before and gazed into space as if in shock. Had Mrs Garside spoken the truth? Had she really altered so much? She thought about the changes Lizzie had brought into her life and how she had wanted to cope without anyone's help. She had wanted them all to realise that she could be as good a mother as anyone could be, but slowly as realisation soaked into her being, she understood how she had alienated the people who loved her the most. At first she wanted to reject the charges brought against her, but Mrs Garside was right, of course. She had been selfish in her attitude to all concerned and thought only of fulfilling her main ambition, to be a mother to Lizzie.

Guilt overwhelmed her as she thought of Laura's loneliness since George had died and how she had been so anxious to get away on the few occasions she had visited her. Then there was Chris. Dear old faithful Chris, whom she had pushed away as surely as if she had physically slammed the door in his face. She would have to go and see him. This couldn't wait - he was far too important to her not to let him know how much she loved him. She thought of the weeks and months that had passed without any physical contact between them, how she had moved out of their bedroom without giving him one moment's thought and was ashamed.

Dashing up the stairs she knocked on Mrs Garside's door.

"Come in." The older woman was sitting in a chair by her bed reading.

"Mrs Garside, I'm sorry. I can't say more at the moment, but I will tomorrow. I want to go and meet Chris from his meeting at the school. Will you listen out for Lizzie for me? She doesn't usually wake up, but if she does, well...... will you look after her for me, please. I won't be long."

"Off you go. Lizzie will be fine with me." Mrs Garside smiled, thankful that she had managed to get through to her.

Grabbing her coat as she left the house, Polly hurried along to the school, hoping that she might meet Chris on the way. She didn't know which route he took but he didn't usually get home until well after ten o'clock. At least she thought he did. Her shame was all the greater as she realised she didn't even know when he got in, or left in the morning come to that.

It was eight thirty when she arrived at the school and found it in darkness. She stood around for a few minutes and then decided to knock on the door of the school house to see if he was there.

Mrs Ross answered the door, "Hello," she said kindly, "can I help you?"

"I'm Polly Beauchamp, Mrs Ross. I was wondering if my husband has left the meeting yet."

"The meeting finished about an hour ago, Mrs Beauchamp. He left with Miss Carlisle. I think he was going to see her home. She's not keen on wandering the streets in the dark and your husband always sees her safely home. He's a very thoughtful young man."

Polly looked taken aback, "Yes," she stammered, "he is very thoughtful. Thank you." She was just about to turn away when she asked, "Can you tell me where Miss Carlisle lives and I'll see if he's still there?"

"Yes, of course. She lives on Priestgate in one of the small houses there, but I'm afraid I don't know the number."

Polly's heart was racing as the implications sank in. How long had Chris known this Miss Carlisle? He must have known her for some time if he always saw her home. Why had it taken him so long to get home tonight if the meeting had finished an hour ago? She hurried away, tears stinging her eyes as she went, the keen wind made her pull her coat closer to her body. Her heart was in her mouth as she approached the turning into Priestgate and began walking along the ancient cobbled surface. Most of the windows had their curtains closed against the darkness so she was still no nearer to finding the house she was looking for. She walked back again towards the junction of King Street and George Street, and was just about to turn to walk back yet again, when she spotted two figures emerging from the George Hotel at the top of the road. They were indistinguishable from where she was standing, but as they approached she breathed a huge sigh of relief as she recognised Chris. She raised her hand to wave but then noticed that the woman had her arm through his and they were leaning towards each other with an air of intimacy as they talked and laughed. It had been a long time since she had been that way with Chris, and the barbs of jealously stabbed at her. She didn't know what to do so she stepped back into the dimly lit street and crossed the road. She slipped into a passageway which served two of the houses and waited for the figures to come to her. She watched as they arrived at the house opposite and noticed how pretty the young woman was. Surely Chris wasn't seeing her, was he? If she was honest with herself, she wouldn't blame him, but hoped and prayed that he wasn't.

The woman, who she now knew as Miss Carlisle, took out her keys and Polly held her breath as she opened the door and stepped in. She heard her tinkling laughter as she held the door open and said something to Chris. He looked at his watch and shook his head in answer to her question. She saw the woman shrug her shoulders and close the door, leaving Chris on the doorstep.

She watched as he stood looking at the door for a full three minutes before moving away, shaking his head and she released the breath she had been holding knowing that her fears were unfounded. He might have been tempted, and who could blame him after what she had put him through, but he had walked away. For that she said a prayer of thanks.

She let him get to the end of Priestgate before running up behind him shouting his name. He turned in alarm when he saw it was her.

"What's the matter, Polly? Is Lizzie alright? Has something happened?"

He caught her by the shoulders and held her away from him, searching her eyes for answers.

"No, nothing's wrong, Chris. In fact, things couldn't be better. Let's go home I've a lot to talk to you about," she smiled at him for the first time in months and his face relaxed as he smiled back. It had taken a long time but his Polly was back with him and he knew the long wait had been worth it. He drew her into his arms and they walked home together. Jenny Carlisle's charms faded into insignificance. They talked for hours that evening and made plans for their future. Polly moved back into the marital bedroom and life regained an even keel while Mrs Garside congratulated herself on her success.

***

Jenny Carlisle assumed an air of indifference after Chris's announcement that he wouldn't be able to accompany her for anymore after-meeting drinks. The fact that she seemed not to care whether or not he paid any attention to her confused him greatly. In fact, Miss Carlisle decided that she would be leaving at the end of the next term and moving to another, more modern school, better suited to her individual and progressive ideas.

Chris's relief was tangible.

EIGHTEEN

The sun was scorching hot, blazing from the bluest of skies, and causing heat shimmers on the horizon. The figure riding the chestnut horse seemed to relish the heat and the exercise. He pulled his mount to a halt momentarily at the top of a rise and looked down into the valley below. All he could see for miles was sheep and grass. He took off his hat and wiping his brow, reached for his water bottle which hung from the pommel on his saddle. Taking a long draught and wiping his mouth on his sleeve he dismounted and from a leather pouch pulled out a large cloth holding his sandwiches. He led the horse to the shade of a solitary tree, gnarled but still in leaf, affording both animal and rider the shelter they needed.

Martin Beauchamp loved Australia, he loved the wide open spaces and the freedom of movement, but still he thought of home and wondered how his family were faring, and of course, Laura. His heart turned over when he thought of her and knew that no matter how he tried, how much he pushed his body to the extremes, he still wanted her.

He had been in this country of heat, flies and exotic creatures for almost two years, following up an invitation from one of his Australian pals who he had met in the army. Since then he had learned from his friend, Andy, much of what he needed to know about running a sheep farm, and a great deal of it was learned the hard way. He had faced bush fires, drought, hostility and homesickness, but nothing had discouraged him. This, he thought, was the life he needed to live, but not always as a drover, one day he wanted to own his own sheep farm.

He finished his sandwiches - huge doorsteps of bread filled with cheese, and took another mouthful of water from his bottle. His horse was snuffling in its nosebag and Martin knew it would need a drink too. He stood up and brushed crumbs from his shirt front and removed the nosebag from the horse, speaking to it and gently stroking its neck. The horse snickered and rubbed its head against his arm.

"Come on then, Flash. Let's go and get you some water."

Flash nodded his head displaying the white markings on his forehead which gave him his name. Martin threw himself over the saddle in one easy movement and pulled the reins around, directing his horse down to the valley floor where the stream meandered gently, providing water for both them, the sheep, and irrigating the fields on either side.

Flash stopped abruptly at the bottom and drank thirstily while Martin dismounted once more and watched as his horse paddled and drank in the water. He refilled his water bottle and remembered how the stream wasn't always as docile as it was now. In the rainy season it could swell to three times its width and many a time sheep were left stranded or drowned if they were too slow or too stupid to move quickly.

Eventually, Flash had had his fill and Martin re-mounted. Horse and rider moved as one as they followed the course of the stream for a while. The rider though, had a decision to make, and it was one he knew would change the course of his life and impact on others too. By the time they reached the farmhouse his mind was made up. He would write to Chris and let him know where he was. The rest he would leave to fate.

**

Laura drew the blinds down in the front window of her small shop, *'Taylor Made'*. She had come a long way since that fateful day when George had died so suddenly. She turned around checking to make sure everything was in place for the busiest day of the week, Saturday. She smiled to herself as she saw that everything was tidy and moved to the front door to lock up for the night.

After a great deal of thought, she had invested the money George had left her in this haberdashery and dressmaking business and was delighted when it had become such a success. The stock was varied and she catered for a wide range of clientele and was often asked to make dresses for those who wanted an exclusive design.

It was six o'clock before she reached The Elms, and Emma and Lizzie would have eaten their tea by now in the warm kitchen. She entered as usual through the back door and found both children sitting at the kitchen table colouring in their books with crayons. Emma had grown into a tall young girl and towered over most of her classmates. Lizzie was now three years old and into everything but was still the apple of her parent's eyes.

"Hello, mam. We're just doing some colouring in," Emma smiled.

"Come and see, Aunty Laura," Lizzie joined in.

Laura went over and admired their handiwork. "I'm just going to see your Aunty Polly, Emma. I won't be long. You carry on with your crayoning."

She climbed the few steps into the hallway and knocked on the sitting room door before entering. Polly and Chris were sitting in their fireside chairs and so Laura sat on the sofa directly between them.

"Had a good day?" Polly asked, as she finished a row of knitting.

"Not too bad, thanks."

"We've got some news for you, Laura," Chris said reaching up to the mantelpiece and lifting down a letter. "We've heard from Martin."

Laura held her breath as she stared at the envelope which Chris was holding out to her.

"Go on, have a look at it yourself. It makes interesting reading."

When she had finished she looked at Polly and Chris who were smiling at her reaction.

"I can't believe he's in Australia. I thought he was going to Hong Kong," she exclaimed.

"We were surprised too, weren't we, Polly?" Chris looked over at his wife for her contribution and she nodded obligingly.

"He seems to be doing well though, doesn't he? I don't think he'll be coming back any time soon," she smiled, before noticing Laura's downcast expression.

"Are you writing back, Chris?" Laura asked.

"Yes, of course. We haven't heard from him for years so he'll want to know our news as well."

Laura looked flustered, "Well, give him my best wishes, won't you?"

"I certainly will."

Emma appeared at that moment carrying her coat and scarf. "Are we going home now, mam? I feel really tired today. I don't like the cold 'cos it makes my leg ache worse."

"Come on, then. Let's be off." Laura was in fact delighted to be leaving. The letter from Martin had shaken her more than she cared to admit and would be pleased to be home herself. She and Emma still lived in the house in Bowmandale, even though she was financially secure now, and could have moved up in the world if she had wanted to and bought her own home. She had furnished the house to her taste and decoration and she was happy there so saw no point in moving just for the sake of it.

***

Later that evening Laura sat alone, as usual, in front of her fire in the kitchen, toasting her feet while mulling over Martin's letter. He really seemed to be enjoying himself out there and although he had asked about her, he obviously had no idea that she was now a widow, because he also asked about George. She itched to read the letter again, having skipped much of the news it contained because she had felt Chris and Polly watching her and didn't want them to know how thrown she had been. If only she could ask to read it again without sounding desperate, but if she confided in Polly about her feelings for Martin, she would no doubt let it slip to Chris and what good would that do? Martin was thousands of miles away and she would never see him again.

She put her head back and closed her eyes, trying to remember how he had looked three years ago and wondered if he had changed. Her heart leapt as she drew his image in her mind and allowed herself to feel again how wonderful it was to have his arms around her when they were dancing at the Carnival, and how excitingly dangerous it had been when they had almost kissed. She chose to erase the scenes of George and Martin fighting because she just wanted to hold onto something really special. Her heart was aching for the need of him and tears squeezed out of her closed eyes and ran unheeded down her cheeks.

***

Emma went with Laura to the shop the next day and helped by tidying up the drawers which held the buttons, cottons, bias binding, and other sewing accessories. She liked the button drawer best of all and made sure that all the colours and sizes were together in the same compartments.

The bell rang in the front of the shop and Emma heard her Auntie Polly's voice.

"Hello, Laura. I just need some wool to finish that cardigan I'm knitting for Lizzie."

Emma ran into the shop, "I'll get it for you, Auntie Polly."

She looked behind the counter and found the bag with Polly's name on it and removed the remaining balls of wool. "Do you want it all?"

"Yes please, Emma. I'm going to finish it over the weekend I think." Polly looked at Laura, "You certainly have a willing helper here on a Saturday, don't you?"

Laura smiled, "I don't know what I'd do without her. She's a marvel at keeping things tidy."

Emma strutted importantly, pleased at the compliments being paid to her, much to the other two women's amusement.

"Would you like to go and fetch some sweets?" Polly asked innocently, "and while you're out you can pick up some iced fingers from the cake shop next door."

Emma looked at her mother for permission and Laura nodded. "We'll have a cup of tea in the back while it's quiet. I'm closing up at 12 o'clock for half an hour anyway."

When Emma had left the shop, Laura put the 'Closed' sign up as she always did on a Saturday and pulled the curtain aside for Polly to go through to the back room which housed a tiny kitchen. There was a square brown table to one side, and on a small worktop next to the sink was a gas ring just big enough to hold a kettle.

"Have you left Lizzie with Chris?" Laura asked.

"Yes, he looks forward to playing with her at the weekend. I can't tell you how things have changed since I came to my senses. We're so happy, Laura, and guess what – I think I'm having another baby."

Laura looked concerned, "Oh, Polly. I'm pleased for you, of course, but I thought the doctor said you weren't supposed to have any more after Lizzie."

"Well, maybe it'll be different this time. I'm going to see him next week. Anyway, I've brought you something."

Laura watched expectantly as Polly delved into her shopping bag, and took a deep breath when she handed her Martin's letter.

"I didn't think you could have read it properly last night, so I thought you'd like to have more time to read it. Chris says it's alright for you to keep it over the weekend and he'll reply next week."

"What makes you think I need to read it again?" Laura asked, feeling her face redden as she spoke.

"Oh, come off it, Laura. It's obvious that Martin means a lot to you. He always has done – well, for years now anyway."

Laura's face was like a beetroot and she turned away to see to the kettle and make their tea.

"Don't be embarrassed. It's lovely that you like him. It's been a long time since George died and you're only young. Is it because of Martin that you've never bothered with anyone else?"

Laura brought the teapot over to the table and recovered herself before answering truthfully, "Partly, I suppose. But partly because I've been so busy with trying to get this business off the ground and looking after Emma. It's not easy being alone. I don't know what I would have done without the money George left me in that insurance policy."

"You could have come and stayed with us, of course."

"You were too wrapped up in Lizzie at the time if you remember."

"Oh, yes. Sorry, Laura. I really wasn't myself then was I?" It was Polly's turn to be embarrassed.

"Thanks for bringing me the letter. I'll read it tonight and bring it over tomorrow when we come for dinner."

"Chris wondered if you wanted to put a letter in with his when he writes back."

"I'll think about it."

At that moment, Emma came in the back door carrying a bag of iced fingers which they shared out amongst themselves and the conversation moved on to general matters.

After Polly had gone and she opened the shop again for business, the afternoon sped by as a constant flow of people passed through, which kept Laura's mind too busy to think of the letter which was waiting to be re-read that evening.

***

Again, that evening when Emma was asleep, Laura sat at the table and read the letter three times more. Martin certainly sounded as if he was having a wonderful time on the sheep farm and she noted that he would like to settle out in Australia and buy a farm of his own. Her mouth turned down at the corners as she realised that this meant he hadn't given any thought to returning to England, and never would if he bought a farm out there.

By the time she had mulled over everything he had written, she came to the conclusion that she would not write to him. He had made his life out there and appeared to be happy. What would be the point in contacting him now – she doubted he would thank her for it. In any case, he probably had someone else to share his life with, although he hadn't mentioned anyone in his letter. He was a man after all so she doubted he would have remained without female company for three years. No, even though she wanted him to come home, it wouldn't be fair to put any pressure on him to do so.

***

Polly's visit to the doctor a few days later caused her to panic. After her examination he looked over his glasses at her saying, "You're not expecting again, Polly, but I would like to send you to the hospital for a check-up. You might need an operation."

"Operation?" Polly was horrified. "What for?"

"There may be a problem with your uterus, it may be fibroids, but we'll know more after some tests are done. In the meantime, I want to prescribe some tablets which might take away some of the pain you've been experiencing."

Polly left the surgery thinking of how disappointed Chris would be if she couldn't accompany him to Australia later in the year so she decided not to tell him about her visit to the doctor. She hadn't told him about her suspicions of pregnancy anyway, so she would leave him in blissful ignorance.

NINETEEN

The Faraday sheep farm where Martin had lived and worked for the past two years was situated approximately three hours ride away from Melbourne, so the post was slow in arriving and was usually picked up by one of the family when they went into town for supplies. It was no wonder then, that he didn't get his letter from Chris until eight weeks after it had been posted, and then it was delivered by the Flying Doctor Service when he came out to visit Andy's wife, Joan, who was six months pregnant with their first child.

Martin met the doctor at the makeshift landing strip and drove him to the house. He took the bag and sorted out the mail before delivering it to the other workers in the bunk house. When he saw the fat, white envelope from Chris he walked to the water's edge and sat down to read it in peace. He was disappointed to note that Laura had not written to him separately, but almost dropped the letter when he read that George had died not long after he had started out on his travels. He stood up and walked up and down the river bank, cursing his stupidity in staying out of touch for so long.

He stopped in his tracks when, further into the letter, he read that Laura was now a successful business woman in the town thanks to a legacy from George, and slowly it dawned on him that she might not need him anymore. He had been stupid to moon around the place thinking of her night after night, wondering if she was happy. He let the hand holding the letter fall to his side. He felt like a teenager who had been stood up on his first date. Laura was probably having a high old time of it, living it up on her new found wealth.

He started to read again but his thoughts kept returning to Laura so he decided to saddle up Flash and go into Melbourne and visit the agent who was selling a farm he had heard of in a more remote area. Walking back to the farmhouse, he saw Andy was about to drive the doctor back to the plane.

"Hey, Andy, I'll run the doc back. Can I borrow the 'ute' for a couple of days? I need to go into Melbourne and I'll bring it back when I've finished some business. It'll be quicker than taking Flash."

"Yeah, mate. No problems. Fill up the spare tanks, will ya?"

"You bet."

Martin grabbed a few things together and stuffed them into a canvas bag before joining the doctor and running him out to the landing strip. He then carried on to what passed as a main road, but was in fact mostly a dirt track, and headed into Melbourne. The empty petrol cans jostled for position in the back of the truck but he was pleased to note that there was enough water to see him through the day.

His journey took him the rest of the day to complete but by early evening he had arrived at the hotel where he booked in for a couple of nights. After checking in and stashing his bag in his room, he went to the agent who was selling the property he had been considering and made an appointment to view it first thing the next day.

The hotel was unassuming but the food was good and plentiful, so after dinner that evening he had a couple of drinks at the bar and then went to his room. His excitement was tempered by the disappointment that Laura was no longer an option and he recognised that he had been living his life hoping that one day they could be together. He opened the letter from Chris which he had packed hastily with his clothes and lay on his bed to read it again. The letter dropped out of his hands in no time as sleep overcame him.

Bright and early the next day he drove out with the agent to view the old Carmichael place which had at one time been a successful sheep farm, and after careful consideration and viewing the shearing sheds and worker's accommodation he signed on the dotted line. He was now the owner of a sheep farm. Old Mr Carmichael had died at the grand old age of eighty five and his family wanted rid of the place so that they could get on with their lives. He had two sons, both of whom had farms of their own and didn't want the extra acreage. So, Martin bagged himself a bargain and thirty-five thousand acres of prime sheep and cattle rearing land. The farmhouse itself needed modernising and would take a fair bit of money to renovate but Martin's wages were mostly untouched and sat in his bank account, steadily gaining interest.

His eyes fell on the envelope on the bedside table and he couldn't resist reading it again, hoping against hope that he would see something different in it as far as Laura was concerned. He had dreamed of her in the minutes prior to waking and her smile lingered in his memory even through the years and miles of separation, she still had the power to arouse him. Perhaps he had been too hasty in thinking she wouldn't be interested in him anymore. What if – but no. He would write back to Chris telling him that he had bought the farm and invite him and Polly to come out for a visit when they could get away. He might include Laura in the invitation – at least that way if she refused to come over, he would know where he stood.

***

The following day Martin arrived back at the Faraday farm and broke the news of his purchase to Andy.

"Aw, mate, what am I gonna do without ya? You're one of the family don't ya know that? If I'd known you were gonna go and get your own place I'd never had let you borrow the 'ute'."

Martin laughed and slapped his friend on the back. "Don't give me that. You can manage quite well without me. Anyway, you've known I've wanted a place of my own for ages."

"Yeah, I know, but it's kinda hard knowing you won't be on hand when I need someone trustworthy."

"You'll be able to radio me. I'll have the one that's in the place up-dated, it looks like Noah might have used it."

"Well, you'd better come in and tell Joanie what you've gone and done. She'll not like it, mate, not one bit."

"I'm not leaving for a month or two. I'll wait till things have quietened down a bit and then I'll go. I hope you'll come with me to the markets to help me stock my place. I'm thinking of cattle and sheep."

"'Course I will. I think me and Joanie will want to give the place the once over."

"That's settled then."

***

Martin had been installed in his new home for eight months and thanks to Andy, he had new stock and had hand-picked his workers for their knowledge, strength and loyalty. Joanie had thrown herself into re-designing his kitchen and, knowing very little about such things, he had let her have her way. It was Joanie who chose his cook, a middle-aged woman whose husband would be useful doing odd-jobs around the place and Andy promised to send the itinerant shearers along once his sheep had been shorn. The worker's accommodation was full of men who knew sheep and cattle like their own kin so Martin was overjoyed when, after six months, the place looked like a new pin. The renovations had happened before his eyes with speed and skill and he could only marvel at Joanie's enthusiasm and energy especially when she gave birth to Andy's son and then re-appeared a week later to finish overseeing the work on the house. Watching his friend and his wife with their new baby, Martin knew a sense of loss greater than he would have thought himself capable.

Catching his eye, Andy said, "It's about time you settled down, and found yourself a woman, mate. I can recommend it."

"I can see that," was the only reply. Joanie smiled a smile of utter contentment and Martin was again reminded of Laura.

That night he wrote to Chris.

TWENTY

"We've had another letter, Laura," Polly enthused as she watched for her sister's reaction.

"Another letter?" Laura asked, trying and failing to convey her disinterest.

Polly drummed her fingers on the counter top in agitation, "Yes, from Martin. Don't pretend you don't know who I mean."

Laura took a deep breath and turned to face her sister. "It's hopeless, Polly. He's obviously not interested in me or he would have written separately. I'm presuming Chris told him about George's accident?"

"Yes, but he's had a lot on. He's bought a sheep farm and wants us to go and see him."

Laura's eyes lit up, "What? All of us, or just you, Chris and Lizzie?"

"He said you can come too if you want to. We're thinking about going over for the whole six weeks of the school summer holidays. You can get an aeroplane now that takes only four days to get there."

"And Emma and me can come if we want to? Doesn't sound very tempting when it's put like that."

"You're just being stand-offish now because he hasn't written directly to you."

"Well, what makes you think he even wants me out there?"

"Because I saw how you both were before he left, Laura. I think you'll make a lovely couple. He's not married yet and I don't think he's got anybody in mind either."

Laura's face fell, "Oh, I don't know, Polly. Let me think about it. It means getting someone in to look after the shop for me and everything. Six weeks is a very long time."

"He won't wait forever, Laura."

Polly turned on her heels and left the shop. It was half-day closing and Laura needed to think so she pulled down the blinds and put the 'Closed' sign in the window. The news Polly had imparted had affected her more than she cared to admit, but to leave her business for six weeks and travel thousands of miles to Australia was quite a leap for someone who had hardly ever been out of Lincolnshire.

***

It had become a family tradition that Laura and Emma would eat Sunday lunch at the Elms, and the Sunday following Polly's visit to the shop was no exception. The conversation was all about the proposed visit to Australia. Mrs Garside kept her own counsel and said very little.

"We're taking the Kangaroo Route, Laura. We'll be there in four days. Can you believe it? Thousands of miles in four days – I thought I'd never want to leave Barton again when we came back from Canada, but I think I'm ready for another adventure." Polly's excitement was evident to everyone.

Laura couldn't help but show an interest in all the plans and was just a little bit envious of her sister's adventurous spirit.

"Why don't you think about coming with us?" Chris pleaded with her. "I'm sure Martin would be overjoyed if you came too."

"I don't know where you get that idea from," she replied looking sideways at Emma who was unusually silent.

Polly noticed the glance and decided to capitalise on it. "You'd like to come with us, wouldn't you Emma?"

Emma looked up from her plate and shook her head. "Only if mam wants to go. I just want her to be happy."

"Out of the mouths of babes," Chris said, looking pointedly at Laura.

"We'll talk about it tonight, just the two of us, shall we, Emma?"

"Alright. Can I have some more potatoes please?"

***

Polly was woken in the night by terrible cramping pains in her stomach. She reached for the tablets which the doctor had given her. She kept them in her bedside drawer and usually managed to take them without Chris's knowledge. This time though, she was out of luck as he switched the light on just as she found the bottle.

"What's the matter, Polly? You don't look very well." His concern was evident as he reached out to hold her hand.

"I've just got a pain in my stomach, that's all."

He noticed the tablets and reached out to take them. "What're these for?"

"The doctor gave them to me," she replied hesitantly, knowing she should have told him what the doctor had said.

"I think you'd better explain."

She sat up and took a tablet, waiting for the pains to settle before answering.

When she finished telling him about the pains and the doctor's diagnosis Chris was torn between anger and alarm.

"Why didn't you tell me before?"

"I didn't want to worry you unnecessarily. The doctor is going to send me to the hospital so that I can have an examination."

"When's your appointment?"

"Next Tuesday afternoon, but I can drive myself there. There's no need for you to come with me."

"I'm coming whether you want me to or not. I'll see about getting the afternoon off. I'll leave some work for the children to do so it'll just mean someone sitting with them. What time's the appointment?"

"Half past two."

Chris looked at his wife whose pallor had now returned to something near normal.

"Are you still in pain?"

"No, it's worn off now. Put the light out and we'll get some sleep, eh?"

Within an hour of Chris falling asleep again, Polly was heaving over the toilet basin, the pains having returned ten-fold. Chris heard her and rushed into the bathroom. He took one look at her and ran down the stairs to call for the doctor, who arrived within ten minutes and ordered an ambulance.

"We need to get you into hospital, Polly. A specialist needs to look at you."

At this point Polly was beyond argument and sat doubled up on the stairs waiting for the transport. It arrived promptly and Mrs Garside was put in charge of

Lizzie with instructions to send for Laura if she needed to.

The following hours were the worst Chris had ever spent in his life, and that included being shot at as a pilot. Polly was rushed into surgery moments after arriving at the hospital and he paced the floor in the waiting room, constantly checking the time with an old clock on the wall. Hour by hour he waited for someone to come and tell him what was going on, but no one did. He tried reading some magazines and read the same posters over and over again, but took nothing in. All he could think about was Polly, and why she had been so stupid as not to have told him about her problem.

Eventually, someone took pity on him and offered him a cup of tea but it was left un-tasted when he saw a doctor approaching.

"Mr Beauchamp?" the man in the white coat asked.

"Yes. How is she, doctor?"

"Shall we sit down?"

Chris sat heavily on the hard bench in the waiting room, dreading but needing to know what was coming next.

"Your wife has had an emergency operation to remove her uterus, I'm afraid. The surgeon is a first-class chap and expects Mrs Beauchamp to make a full recovery eventually. Unfortunately, she has lost a lot of blood and is presently still very ill."

Chris paled at his words. "Can I see her?"

"Not yet, I'm afraid. She is still in the recovery ward. It might be better if you go home as she probably won't recover consciousness until later in the day."

Chris looked at his watch and then at the clock on the wall. It was four thirty in the morning and he had had little sleep."

"Are you sure she'll be alright, doctor? I would really like to see her if possible, just to make sure for my own sake."

"As I said, it's impossible at the moment, but if you come back later, after lunch perhaps, she'll be awake."

"If you're sure," he looked intently into the face of the doctor but could glean nothing from his expression. "Alright, I'll go, but if she wakes up or anything happens, please leave instructions for someone to telephone me. I've filled the forms out and my number is on there."

"Don't worry, Mr Beauchamp. Go home and get some rest. You'll feel better."

Chris walked on wobbly legs as he thought of Polly lying somewhere in the building not knowing he had gone home. "Will someone tell my wife that I'll be in to see her later?"

"I'll leave instructions with the Ward Sister."

He nodded and turned to leave. His thoughts were on his wife and he felt numb with worry. How could things change so quickly? With slumped shoulders and head bowed he tried to imagine his life without Polly – and couldn't.

***

Laura insisted on closing her shop when she found out about Polly's operation and accompanied Chris to the hospital that same afternoon. They asked for directions to the ward and were sent upstairs. They had to wait with other people for a while before the doors were opened to allow visitors in but Chris was devastated to learn that Polly still hadn't woken up.

"Your wife's temperature is still very high, Mr Beauchamp but we are doing all we can to bring it down. I'm sure she will wake up shortly." The Ward Sister was firm but kind in her approach but Laura's heart began to race when she saw that there was one bed curtained off from the rest.

"Can we see her now, Sister?" Chris asked, almost afraid of the answer.

"You can sit with her for a few minutes but that's all. We're waiting to do some more tests."

The Sister signalled to a nurse who scurried over. "Nurse, please show Mr Beauchamp and this lady to Mrs Beauchamp's bedside. Five minutes and no more."

"Yes, Sister." She looked at Chris and Laura, "Will you come this way please?"

She led them down to the curtained off bed and indicated that they should go in. Polly's face was flushed with temperature and she lay on her back deathly still. Chris sat down on the chair beside the bed and held her hand, which was icy to the touch. Laura struggled to hold in her tears and took up position on a chair at the other side of the bed, looking down and staying silent.

Chris began talking to Polly hoping for a reaction but he was out of luck. Laura steeled herself to feel Polly's forehead and withdrew her hand a second later, fearful of the heat and dryness of her sister's skin. They had only just settled themselves when the Sister returned and told them their five minutes were up.

"Not yet, surely!" Chris couldn't help the annoyance penetrating his voice.

"The doctor would like to speak to you, Mr Beauchamp. He's waiting in my office if you'd like to see him there."

Chris's heart sank even further and he pushed himself up and followed the Sister back up the ward while Laura sat in a corridor.

Half an hour later Laura was pacing the floor when Chris returned looking ghostly white.

"What is it, Chris? What did the doctor say?"

"He said that she has septicaemia and she's really poorly."

Laura watched as Chris slumped onto one of the chairs she had vacated and buried his face in his handkerchief. Immediately, she was by his side and patted his back comfortingly while he tried to regain his composure.

"Try and stay strong for Polly's sake, Chris. She'll need you to look after her when she comes home."

Chris nodded and blew his nose, "Sorry, Laura. It's been such a horrendous shock. I didn't even know she'd been to the doctors until last night."

"Come on, let's go back home. We'll keep in touch by telephone and come back tomorrow."

Chris allowed himself to be led away and by the time they reached the car he had recovered himself sufficiently to drive back home.

Chris had sent a telegram to Martin to let him know how things stood and he was unsure as to whether or not they would make it to Australia in August and Martin had replied sending his love to Polly for a speedy recovery.

TWENTY ONE

It was three days before Polly woke from her deep sleep. The drugs to reduce her temperature and overcome her infection worked together to keep her sedated. A drip hung at the side of the bed making sure her body was hydrated while the staff diligently checked her responses every hour. Her wound was dressed regularly and the infection appeared to be dissipating.

Chris was by her bedside when she opened her eyes and he immediately leaned over and whispered her name. She blinked as full consciousness seeped into her brain and tried to speak but her voice rasped in her dry throat. As she coughed to try and clear it she winced as pain shot through her abdomen and Chris nervously called for a nurse.

He was led away from her bed while the medical staff attended to Polly and a doctor was called to examine her. Chris found himself pacing the corridor outside the ward oblivious to the half-tiled walls echoing to his footsteps on the well-scrubbed floor. Eventually, the doctor came back and pronounced Polly 'over the worst' and allowed Chris back into the ward.

His heart pounding with anticipation he approached her bed and watched as she smiled up at him, his relief showing in his face.

"Hello, my love. How are you feeling now?"

"I'm not sure. I think I'm alright but I don't remember anything. They said I've had an operation – how long have I been here?"

"Oh, three or four days. But I'm so relieved to see you're awake again. I thought...." His voice broke as his emotions threatened to overwhelm him again.

Polly reached out and touched his hand. "I'm alright now, Chris. It won't be long before I'm home."

Chris swallowed hard. "I know, but I just felt so alone without you. Nothing seemed the right way up – do you know what I mean?"

Polly nodded and gripped his hand tighter to reassure him. "How's Lizzie? Is she alright? I hope she's not frightened is she?"

"No, Laura, Emma and Mrs Garside have done a sterling job looking after her after school. Everyone will be so pleased to hear you are back in the land of the living."

He could see that she was tired and looked around to see that Sister was heading in their direction.

"I think I'd better leave you to get some proper rest now, Polly. I'll be back later tonight with Laura. She'll be really happy to see you're on the mend."

Polly nodded sleepily as Sister reached her beside.

"It's time you left your wife to rest now, Mr Beauchamp. Come along, visiting time is over for now."

Chris rose to his feet and leaned over to kiss Polly's forehead but her eyes were closed once more. He could see that her temperature had lowered and she was sleeping peacefully. There was a new spring in his step as he walked away.

***

"Peggy, I wonder if you would mind working every afternoon this week, instead of your usual three? I want to be at The Elms when Polly comes out of hospital but I'm not sure which day it will be."

Peggy Sutcliffe beamed at Laura, "Of course. I'll work full days if you want me to, as I really need the cash at the moment. We desperately need a new three piece suite and I've seen a lovely one in Thompson's."

Laura had engaged Peggy when her working hours were badly affected by Polly's illness. With looking after Lizzie and Emma as well as dressmaking for her more discerning customers, she found her time was more in demand than usual. Mrs Garfield did her best but she was getting on a bit now and cooking for the family was enough for her these days. Indeed, she wondered how the old lady kept going at all and would not be at all surprised if she announced her retirement any day.

Looking over at Peggy Sutcliffe she realised for the first time how young she looked. Her trim figure and fashionable hair-do made Laura feel middle-aged and with a shock she remembered she would be thirty-six in a few weeks time. Peggy was a newly-wed youngster of twenty-one, her bubbly personality overflowed as she enthused about everything. It had been the main factor why Laura had chosen her after being interviewed for the position of Assistant and had never been disappointed with her decision.

Polly had been in hospital for two months and in that time Peggy had proved herself capable of handling any situation that occurred on a day to day basis in the small shop, so Laura was content to leave her in charge for half a day at a time at least, and Peggy was more than happy to show how efficient she could be.

"Do you want your elevenses, Mrs Taylor?" Peggy asked.

"I think we could both do with a break, don't you?" Laura replied, thinking how quickly Peggy had settled in. She had only been at the shop since Polly was taken ill but in that time had become indispensable.

Peggy went into the kitchen at the back as the little bell on the shop door tinkled. Laura, who had just turned around to tidy one of the drawers, turned again to greet her customer. Her eyes widened with shock when she saw who was standing as large as life on the other side of the counter.

"Hello, Laura."

"Martin!" She gasped her face white with the shock of seeing him again.

"You look as if you've seen a ghost," he laughed.

Laura stood behind the counter unable to think of what to say, her right hand moving to her throat as she stared at him.

"You've certainly surprised me, that's for sure - what are you doing here?"

"I thought I'd better come over and see how Chris was doing without Polly to keep him in order." The same easy smile lit his face and Laura took in his tall, muscular frame and tanned skin. He looked even more handsome than she remembered and her heart began to pound in her chest.

"Hrrhm." Both Martin and Laura turned to see Peggy standing with two cups of tea in her hand, not really sure if she should be interrupting.

"Oh, Peggy, thank you," Laura said, "this is Martin Beauchamp, my sister Polly's brother-in-law. Martin, this is Peggy who takes over when I'm not around."

Martin smiled in Peggy's direction and she answered, "Pleased to meet you, Mr Beauchamp. Would you like a cup of tea?"

Laura moved to take her tea cup from Peggy saying, "Will you watch the shop for me, Peggy?"

Peggy noticed Laura's flushed face and wondered about her employer and this particularly handsome man.

A few minutes later both Laura and Martin were sat at the small table in the kitchen. Laura's first tongue-tied sentences were soon overcome as he put her at her ease and chatted about Australia and talked enthusiastically about his new home and the people he worked with.

"You've done very well for yourself too, Laura. This is a nice little shop and in a good position."

"Yes, it's been hard work but very worth it."

"How's Emma doing at school? She must be nearly grown up now."

"She's doing very well but she's still a child at heart even though she likes to pretend she's more grown up than she actually is, especially when she's with Lizzie. She mothers her and is quite bossy if she gets the chance."

Martin laughed and Laura saw that he had changed little in himself. His outward appearance might be lean and tanned but inside he was still the Martin she had loved all those years ago.

"Have you been to the Elms?" she asked.

"Yes, I've just dropped my things off. Mrs Garside is still there I see, but she's looking a bit tired and I think it's time she retired."

"I know what you mean. I wouldn't be surprised to hear she was hanging up her pinny at any time."

Martin laughed at Laura's words and without thinking, reached for her hand across the table.

"I've missed you, Laura," he said unexpectedly.

Laura gazed at his large hand as it covered hers and felt herself tremble at his touch, but made no move. She lifted her gaze to look into his eyes which spoke volumes to her.

"I've missed you too, Martin," she whispered, hardly trusting herself to speak. "I thought you'd forgotten about me."

"Forgotten about you – are you daft woman? I had no idea about George's accident until three years after it had happened and then with one thing or another it's taken me this long to pluck up the courage to come back and see whether there's still a chance we might make a go of it. I could kick myself for not staying in touch, but I thought I was doing it for the best."

Laura withdrew her hand from beneath his and sat with both hands in her lap, looking down at them while she tried to gather her scattered senses. She could feel him watching her intently, waiting for some sign that he hadn't returned in vain. Eventually, he could stand the silence no longer and made a move to stand up.

"I'm sorry for springing this on you, Laura and turning up like a bad penny. You've obviously got a lot of things on your mind so I'll go back to The Elms."

"No! Don't go, Martin. I'm sorry – you're right – I do have a lot of things to think about, but I'd rather you stayed with me and helped me to make sense of everything." She smiled as she spoke hoping he would understand.

"Let's go out for the afternoon," he said on impulse, holding out his hand to her.

"I can't, Polly's coming out of hospital this week and I promised Chris I'd make sure everything is ready for her."

"Well, what are you waiting for then? Let's be off."

This time he did stand up and pulled her up with him, holding her close. She could feel his taut body through his light blazer and remembered the last time she had been this close to him, all those years ago.

Peggy gave a wry smile as they walked out of the front door arm in arm.

TWENTY TWO

After two months in hospital Polly was pleased to be home. Everywhere had been cleaned and looked like a new pin. She was glad to see Lizzie looking cheerful and thanked everyone for their efforts in keeping everything ticking along.

She was more than happy to see that Martin and Laura were getting along once more and she could see the contentment on Laura's face. Emma, too, seemed to be relaxed in his company and Chris was delighted with everything. Mrs Garside worried her though, so she decided to speak to Chris about the changes she'd seen in her since she had been back from hospital.

"It's as if she's grown old while I've been away, or I was so used to seeing her that I didn't realise?" she said one evening when they were alone.

"What do you think we should do about it? You know how fond of everyone she is. It will really upset her to have to leave," Chris pointed out.

"She still has her own house on Caistor Road that she rents out - maybe she could move back in there."

"She's so used to being with us though, she'll be very lonely."

Polly thought about this for a while. "Has your father made provision for her? A pension or something?"

"I don't know. I'll have to write to him and ask."

"Yes, you do that and I'll speak to her about her plans for retirement."

"Who's retiring?" Martin asked as he walked into the sitting room, having heard the end of their conversation.

"We were thinking about Mrs Garside. She's really looking old these days, and tired," Polly answered.

"I noticed that when I first came back."

"Do you know if she has a pension from the family?" Chris asked his brother.

"I believe she has. She won't go hungry after all the years she's looked after us."

"No, I know that, but we don't want her to feel we are putting her out to pasture."

Polly interjected, "You never know, she might have plans of her own."

"That's true," Martin laughed. "She might surprise us all yet."

"I'm going to speak to her now," Polly declared and stood up to leave the room.

"She's just gone up to her room," Martin informed her. "I've just been in the kitchen with her."

"I won't be long. I'll see what she wants to do."

Mrs Garside was just about to sit down in a chair in her room when Polly knocked on the door, so she called "Come in," more impatiently than she intended.

Polly peeped around the door, "Is it alright if I come in and talk to you for a moment?"

"Yes, if you want to. What's the matter?"

"Nothing's the matter I just want to ask you something, that's all."

Polly perched on the end of the bed and realised that she had acted on impulse and didn't know where to begin. Mrs Garside picked up her knitting saying, "Well, spit it out, Polly. What's on your mind that can't wait till tomorrow?"

"We were just talking downstairs and wondered if you had any plans – for the future, I mean."

"You mean am I going to retire soon? Don't bother to deny it I can see it in your face." Mrs Garside continued knitting, not letting her face show her inner smiles.

"I wouldn't put it that way....."

"Well, what way would you put it then?"

Polly squirmed in her discomfort and Mrs Garside relented, laughing. "Eeeh, Polly. I wouldn't have missed the look on your face for a minute, I really wouldn't."

"You're not mad with me for asking then?"

"No, don't be soft. I'd be wondering too if I was you. No one can go on working forever and I'm well overdue some time to myself. In fact, I was going to speak to you about it before you went off to Australia."

"Have you got enough money put by to live on, Mrs Garside? We don't want you to leave us and then end up homeless."

The older woman laughed, "I'm alright in that department, Polly. Sir Giles, bless his heart, has settled a good sum on me, in fact he did that before the war and I haven't touched it. I've got my house to sell too, so I thought I'd find a little cottage by the sea somewhere like Mablethorpe and see out the rest of my days there."

"Won't you be lonely though after being with us for so long?"

"I dare say it'll take some getting used to, but I have relatives in Skegness and I can make new friends, can't I?"

"Looks like you've got it all planned out."

"I thought I'd hand in my notice when you go to Australia for a few months, and then it'll be all tidy like."

"We're not going until Christmas now. My operation put paid to the plan to go in August. Why don't you stay with us for as long as you like. You don't have to do any cooking or anything, just live with us like you do now as one of the family."

"That's very kind, Polly. I'll think it over."

"I'll go and tell the others, shall I?"

"Yes, you do that."

***

Laura sat at home watching as Emma read her new book *'The Secret Garden'* which Martin had bought for her. She was growing into a lovely girl, tall and slim with beautiful big eyes and thick curly hair which she had inherited from her father. Emma looked up and caught Laura watching her.

"What's the matter, mam?" she asked, noting the sad but proud look on her mother's face.

"I was just thinking that's all."

"What about? You look sad."

"No, I'm not sad, far from it. I was just thinking how much like your dad you're getting."

Emma coloured slightly as she accepted the compliment which she knew her mother was paying her. She put her book to one side and decided there and then to ask a question which had been playing on her mind ever since Martin had returned.

"Are you going to marry Martin, mam?"

Laura was taken aback at such a direct question but recovered quickly and smiled. "He hasn't asked me," she replied truthfully.

"Well, would you, if he did?"

"I don't know. What do you think?"

"I think you should. Dad's been gone a long time now and you need somebody."

Laura almost laughed out loud at the grown up words coming from her child, but stopped herself knowing it would hurt Emma if she did.

"When and *if* he asks me I'll talk to you first shall I?" she said, making the answer into a joke.

"No. You've got to do what you think is best. Would he come back here or would we go to live in Australia?"

"I've no idea, love. We've not talked about it."

Emma seemed satisfied with the answers to her questions and standing up said, "I'm going to bed to read now. Night, mam." She leaned over to kiss her mother.

"Night, Emma." Laura replied thoughtfully.

When Emma had gone up to bed Laura went outside and walked up the steps onto the raised garden area which George had kept so tidy when he had been alive. The apple tree was in full leaf and the night air was warm and humid. She strolled down the cinder path which George had laid as a temporary measure so that she could hang her washing out without getting muddy feet. As she walked she thought about Martin and wondered why he hadn't asked her to marry him. He had been home a month now and they had really become close again so why didn't he ask her? Had he decided that he didn't love her enough? Perhaps he just wanted her as a friend or maybe he wanted a mistress. No, Laura knew instinctively that he wasn't like that.

She stopped pacing and looked over the other garden fences. Mr Barley, next-door-but-one, had runner beans growing up a wigwam of sticks and next to them straw and netting keeping the last of the strawberry crop from touching the ground and rotting, or worse, becoming a nice nibble for a slug or two. She liked her home but the home in Australia which Martin had described sounded idyllic. Was he taunting her with stories of its huge kitchen? Did the sun shine nearly every day? The only thing she didn't really like were the stories of the snakes and creepy crawlies – but other people managed, so why couldn't she? Did he think she was too soft?

She took a deep breath and exhaled slowly. Maybe, he just didn't want to uproot her and Emma. She shook her head to disperse her thoughts and turned abruptly when she heard the crunch of someone walking behind her on the cinder path. As if her thoughts had conjured him up, Martin moved towards her and she automatically walked into his outstretched arms.

"Hello. I was just thinking about you," she murmured into his ear.

"I must have read your mind. I have to talk to you, Laura. Shall we go into the house or talk out here?"

Without answering she took his hand and pulled him in the direction of the house. Once inside he sat at the table with the red chenille cloth, which still adorned it, instead of taking the usual fireside chair. Laura's heart sank as she took note of his serious face.

"I've got to go back to Australia, love. I've been here too long now, and Polly is almost back to her usual self. The farm can't run itself and decisions need to be made."

Tears began to invade her eyes as she imagined life without him around again, but drew in a deep breath and blinked them away.

"I see," she said shortly.

"I want you to come with me," he blurted out in the most unromantic way possible and he missed her expression as her body stiffened with tension.

"What? Just like that – without talking about it first." Laura could feel her disappointment turning to anger.

"We have talked about it, haven't we? I've told you all about the sheep station and what the house is like."

"You've never mentioned me giving up my life here and going to live thousands of miles away. Did you think I was so desperate that I would drop everything, my family, my business and my friends, just because you want me to go with you?"

Martin's face fell and the excitement left his eyes; she could see that she had hurt him.

"No, I didn't mean that. It's just that we've been getting on so well and I thought it was understood between us that we would marry and....."

"Marry! Now you want me to marry you without even a proposal? What do you take me for?" her voice was raised enough to penetrate the ceiling where Emma listened from her bed.

"I thought you loved me," Martin threw back at her. "It looks like I was wrong."

"No more than *I* was when I imagined a romantic proposal by moonlight," she countered.

He was about to reply when a movement caught his eye and he saw Emma standing in the doorway with tears running down her cheeks. He was immediately on his feet and swept her up in his arms and she clung to

237

him as her body shook with sobs. Laura looked helplessly on. How could she have been so thoughtless as to forget what Emma had said earlier in the evening?

"Come on settle down, sweetheart," Martin murmured, trying to calm Emma down.

"Give her to me," Laura snapped, but stayed her hand when Emma's grip tightened around Martin's neck.

Martin sat in one of the fireside chairs holding the little girl until her sobs became occasional sniffs into the large handkerchief he had given her.

"Now then – tell us all about it. Did we frighten you?"

"Not frighten...." she began. "I was just worried that you would go away and we wouldn't see you again."

Laura turned away as the importance of her daughter's words struck home. Her little girl loved this man as her father and she had never noticed. The knowledge hurt her more than words and she went to Emma's side and knelt beside her.

"We're sorry, love. We were just having a disagreement and it got a bit loud, didn't it?"

"Yes," Emma nodded, "but I heard you arguing about getting married and I thought you were going to say 'no'."

Martin looked at Laura and interrupted. "I've been a bit silly," he said to Emma. "I forgot to ask your mum properly. Shall I do it now?"

Emma looked tearfully into this man's face and nodded.

"You'll have to let me get up then," he laughed and tickled her to make her smile.

Emma went to sit in another chair and Laura watched as Martin came to stand in front of her. She started to smile and Emma was delighted when he got down on one knee.

"Laura, my darling," he began. He winked at Emma, making her laugh. "Will you marry me? If you accept you will make me the happiest man in the world."

He reached inside his blazer pocket and took out a small box offering it to Laura. She took it from him and opened it up, laughing down at him. The ring inside was perfect, three sapphires and two diamonds twinkled from the velvet interior.

"Martin," she gasped, "this is beautiful."

"Will you marry me, Laura - please answer quickly as my knees have gone numb." His pained expression soon had her laughing again.

Emma clapped her hands in delight as Laura nodded, "Yes, Martin. I'll marry you."

Once on his feet he took the ring and slipped it onto her finger.

"I promise to love you forever, Laura", he said as he kissed her hand.

EPILOGUE

Australia was a revelation to Laura and Emma with the house being just as Martin had described it. The difference between her home in England and the farmstead was total, but it didn't stop her relishing the new challenges which came with her new life, and she never looked back.

Polly and Chris visited once or twice a year and when twin boys were born to Laura and Martin a year after their wedding, Polly was on hand to help with everything. Martin was content and happy in the knowledge that he and his family's futures were secure. Laura had been befriended by Joanie and they were in touch constantly, mostly over the radio. When Laura thought back over her years in England it seemed as if that part of her life belonged to someone else. She still owned the shop on the High Street, but Peggy was now the manageress and working towards a partnership. She had been happy to take on the responsibility when it was offered and the business went from strength to strength.

The twins, David and James, kept Laura busy and she found it a pleasure cooking for the workforce especially in the shearing season when the number of men nearly doubled. Although the work was hard, competitions were held between the men as to who could shear the most sheep in two hours, and she enjoyed the camaraderie of the wives. When Joanie came to help out it seemed like one big party.

There were troubled times of course, the droughts and the flash floods, but these were forgotten in the good times and Emma grew tall and strong, learning to ride and helping with the lambing.

Laura sat out on the veranda one evening watching as Emma and Martin put a new horse through its paces. They had bought it together at the horse fair that day for her daughter's fourteenth birthday. They worked in harmony, step-father and step-daughter, and she thought that even though George had hated Martin, he would have been pleased to see his daughter so happy.

Yes, it was a good life here and one she wouldn't swap with anyone. She had everything she could need, a strong, handsome husband who showed her every love and consideration, and a beautiful, healthy, growing family.

She pulled out a letter she had received from Polly and Chris and opened it carefully. She had purposely kept it until the time when the twins were asleep and she could give it her full attention. She raised her eyebrows when she read about Sir Giles and Lady Beauchamp coming back to live in Barton. Young Michael, Martin and Chris's half-brother, had not returned with his parents as he had settled so well in Canada but would visit as often as he could.

Work had started on the renovations to The Elms which would mean Chris, Polly and Lizzie had more privacy and could live separately from his parents. She knew Martin would be pleased to hear his father and step-mother were back in the family home. There was also mention of them all coming over to visit during the next six week holidays from school.

Mrs Garside had retired to Mablethorpe as she had planned, and was happy there with her relatives close at hand. Polly and Chris had taken Lizzie to visit her and spend the day by the sea.

Laura smiled as she finished reading the letter, content in the knowledge that both of their families were inextricably bound together in love.

THE END

Also by J E Christer

Spindrift

Polly's Small Town War

Lightning Source UK Ltd.
Milton Keynes UK
30 March 2010

152116UK00001B/40/P